Of Love and Leland

A World War II Generation Memoir

by

Susanah Jameson Mayberry

Guild Press of Indiana
Carmel, IN 46032

© Copyright 1997 by Susanah Jameson Mayberry
Cover Art by Nell Revel Smith, Leland, Michigan

ALL RIGHTS RESERVED

No part of this book may be reproduced or utilized in any form or by any means, electronic or mechanical, including photocopying and recording, or by an information storage and retrieval system, without permission in writing from the publisher. The Association of American University Presses' Resolution on Permission constitutes the only exception to this prohibition.

Guild Press of Indiana, Inc.
435 Gradle Drive
Carmel, Indiana 46032
(317) 848-6421

Library of Congress Number 97-71452

ISBN: 1-57860-003-0

For My Daughters
Katherine and Susanah

"Green Acres"— The Jameson cottage.

Of Love and Leland

I have avoided reading autobiographies because the few I did read seem to me to be saying, "me, me, me." Authors blowing their own horns. Here I am though, blowing mine.

I was born in 1921 in Indianapolis and led the life of a privileged child, though it never occurred to me that I was fortunate. When I was growing up, the *Town and Country* magazine did a piece on Indianapolis, and when it listed old families, the Tarkington/Jameson clan was among those fortunately blessed. I am a member of this clan. I've always wondered about "old families." To me, it means that my ancestors came to Indiana a very long time ago and stayed there. My great-great-great grandfather, Reverend Joseph Tarkington, was born in 1800 and died in 1899, so I expect that makes us "old family." He was a Methodist circuit rider. When the snow and ice were deep, the riders put leggings which were a pair of men's trousers upside down on the horses' legs so they wouldn't be too cut up by the ice. That certainly wasn't privileged.

To get to my vital statistics, I am now seventy-five and I have never spent a Christmas away from home. That should say it all. I certainly don't love Indianapolis because of its beauty. It seems to be interminably level, bleak in the winter, hot and dusty in the summer. If I could have two wishes about Indiana, one would be cooler summers and the other, more important, would be a long coast line. I guess it's an impossible wish that Indiana could be like Leland, Michigan. But it has its own assets, of a different sort.

After winters spent with family and school in Indianapolis and wonderful summers at the best spot in Michigan, I graduated from Smith College in 1942. I came home thinking, "World, here I am." Strange to say, the world had other things on its mind besides me, namely, World War II. I went to business school so I could earn my own living. While

8 • Of Love and Leland

I was in this school, I met a lieutenant from Camp Atterbury, Frank Mayberry, and two years later we were married. Frank had to leave me after six weeks of marriage to go and play a much-too-important part in the war in Europe. My brother was navigating a B-17 bomber which flew out of England, so our thoughts settled on survival—for those we loved and ourselves as war brides. Earlier, all had been the bliss of a childhood largely unmarred by trouble.

There were in our generation in our large family, six first cousins. They are now in old age, the children of the nephews who provided copy for Booth Tarkington's *Penrod* stories. We were ordinary, everyday children. Our own lives were happy, I think, and uneventful except we had one thing that only six children have ever had: one of America's favorite authors, Booth Tarkington, was our great-uncle. Our frequent visits with him when he was in Indianapolis provided a kind of exclamation point to our lives. We accepted his magic as children accept most gifts—without questioning. His comings and goings and distinguished guests made the front page, but for us, he was the head of the family, and I think our family's cohesion was increased by his interest in us, and his love for all of us. Did we make the most of our opportunity to love and be loved by such a gracious and important national figure? Probably not, but we certainly had fun.

As I reminisce, I wonder what is the most important thing one person can offer another. Do you think it might be enjoyment? Julian Street wrote about Uncle Booth, "A natural magnetism surrounds this person. Without doing anything or saying a word, he became the center of attention though he never exhibited any consciousness of fame or importance. But this magnetism came about as often as not through his habit of being an absorbed listener." He was a dazzlingly entertaining conversationalist, and he had a store of fascinating, often hilarious, anecdotes about every theatrical and literary celebrity of his day. But when we talked to him, he listened as if what we were saying were the most important thing he had ever heard. This was a considerable part of his great charm. It is impossible to describe him, so I will just ask you if you can imagine in your wildest dreams evening parties, often with three generations, all having the most wonderful fun. This was Uncle Booth in the midst of his family.

If the nephews whose delinquencies had inspired *Penrod* had forgotten to mention them to their children, he saw to it that we were kept informed. Naturally we received those biographical illuminations with pure rapture. There is nothing more satisfying, if you are in trouble over a report card, than to be told that when your father was your age he was in trouble with the police. Not only had our fathers been young once, they had been juvenile delinquents of considerable stature.

We closely watched our fathers during these stories, waiting hopefully for them to show embarrassment or shame. Not at all. They laughed until they cried and interrupted each other in their eagerness to add yet another more horrible story of youthful crime. They seemed proud of having derailed streetcars! Uncle Booth's favorite story was about a summer when my father and uncle tapped into a telephone line behind the barn of the family home at Eleventh and Pennsylvania. They then ordered two quarts of ice-cream to be delivered daily to the porch of a neighbor who was out of town and charged them to him. They stole the ice-cream and went behind the barn to gorge themselves as they talked long distance to their friends at Lake Maxinkuckee, Indiana.

I don't know about my siblings and cousins, but when I was growing up I didn't have the slightest idea that Uncle Booth was a famous and highly respected writer. Actually, I had been looking at something in our library shelves and it had Uncle Booth's name on the front and was inscribed "To Susanah." I didn't read it, but I thought how nice of him it was to talk about me. He could have been out of work, a politician, a salesman or he could have been anything, and it wouldn't have made the slightest difference to the children.

The Tarkingtons went to Kennebunkport, Maine, for six months out of the year, and one Jameson family (ours) went to Leland, Michigan, every summer. When I was four years old, my father had bought a lot right on Lake Leelanau, an inland lake separated from Lake Michigan by road M-22 at Leland and sent up two out-of-work carpenters to build a cottage. They forgot to put in the stairway and the dining room was nine feet too long, but who cared. It became a wonderful, lifelong haven. I have loved that quotation, "unless you were very unlucky as a child, the place you spent your summers was Arcadia." Arcadia in my case was Leland, Michigan.

Of Love and Leland

Probably all over the world there are Lelands. Many lucky people find a way to escape to the woods, the dunes, or the mountains. Russians have dachaus, South Carolinans houseboats which float by river shorelands. Friendship binds these summer experiences together, natural beauty and escape make them indelible in memory. If you see an old friend from your getaway you may not have seen for years, you simply take up just where you left off. Today a treasured experience in Leland is seeing my own granddaughters play in the waves with the grandchildren of old, old friends of mine from early days.

Progress and people have come to Leland, but there are sanctuaries if you know where to look. The little white church is one of them. It has glass windows, not stained, and when they are opened you can hear the bird songs accompanying the hymns. One of our daughters was married there, and the reception was in our front yard. It couldn't rain, so of course it didn't rain.

A few years ago I was chatting with Nell Revel Smith, the painter, who now lives in Leland all the time. I had just finished a novel. She said, "Oh, could I be the first one to read it?"

"Sure," I answered, "but my payment is a painting of my favorite Leland view." I kept my part of the bargain, and so did she. Now I can raise my eyes from my desk in my writing room and see the view from the old ninth hole, looking across the lake.

I think that when we old timers say there are too many cars or people, we should look back and remember some of the things we laughed so hard at years ago. One of them I remember was when Mr. Joyes from Louisville went to the owner of the tacky little grocery store, and told the cross owner that he would like to buy some lemons. "Don't stock lemons no more. Had to quit buying them. They sold too fast." Always Leland was fun.

(l-r) John Tarkington, Donald Jameson, Laurel Tarkington (Booth Tarkington's daughter who died young), Booth Jameson, John Jameson, my father at about age twenty-one.

John and Donald Jameson, age about three to five, dressed in a special outfit by their mother whenever she could get away with it—which was often.

Booth Tarkington at age twenty-eight. Fame awaited him just two short years later.

Quite a few years ago when we were driving down to Indianapolis after our Leland vacation we had a friend of Susie, our daughter, with us. She had been visiting the Stokelys on Lake Michigan. At the stop light at Kessler and Illinois Streets, you could hear and see the noise from the swimming pool at the Riviera Club. Andrea looked sad and said, "The Rivi is so darn dinky after Leland." We all agreed with her.

I have no special memories of my first arrival in Leland, just some incidents of that first summer. In later years, the first sight of Grand Traverse Bay as you come down the long hill on Route 37 meant "We're there." The last twenty-five miles didn't count.

I first remember Leland when I was four in 1925. We were renting one of the Elder Blackledge's log cabins in the Indiana Woods. My family had started coming earlier, though.

Aunt Greenie (Lucile Green) was Mother's closest friend. She married Charles Schaf, and much later they built the cottage which is now "The Retreat" of the John Meads. In 1913, Aunt Greenie was invited to a houseparty in Leland, given by the Bowen girls at Woodbridge Cottage, two doors north of the Millers. Since it was unthinkable for a young lady to travel without a chaperon, her mother went, too. I suppose they took a train to Traverse City, and I think a horse and buggy to Fouch at the far south of Lake Leelanau. Then they went by a steamship, so-called, to Leland. Groceries were also delivered that way.

The Green ladies loved Leland so much that the next year they persuaded Mother and my grandmother to go back to Leland for a vacation with them. They stayed in the hotel on Main Street where the post office is now. After that old hotel burned down, the Nicholas Hotel was built. It's now the Leland Lodge.

A little girl, Peggy Klein, was the daughter of the family who rented Elder Blackledge's other log cabin the first year I was there. Peggy and I were about the same age and best friends. We spent most of our time not on the beach, but in the woods behind the cottages. Parts of it were carpeted with loads of green moss. We built miniature villages with sticks and twig houses held together with strings and matches with green moss floors. I wasn't all that mad for the beach at four years old. Even now I remember Daddy carrying me out screaming into Lake Michigan on a windy day and throwing me into the waves. I guess I must have thought he was throwing me away.

The most scary moment I think I ever had as a child, or maybe at any other time, was that summer. It was a pitch dark night with a howling north wind. Mother and Daddy were out. My brother, Johnny, a baby, was asleep. We had an Irish nursemaid hired when Johnny was born to help out. I was playing with something and didn't know she had left the room. Then at the door came a loud knocking. I opened it. A horrible, bent-over crone, draped in shawls that almost covered her face, said in a cracked scary voice, "Is your Mother home?" I realized when I later read the phrase, "paralyzed with fear" that that's what I was. It was Mary, the nursemaid, playing a joke, or so she thought. I didn't like her very well to begin with because when I accused her once of loving Johnny more than she loved me, she admitted she did. After that night I never could look at her without getting scared all over again. In fact, I wanted to kill her. Later that summer I pulled out a chair she was starting to sit on. I thought it was too bad it didn't hurt her. My father hurt me plenty. I guess she thought the joke was successful, and no, I never told anybody. I was so scared that night that I wet my pants even though paralyzed with fear. Ever since then I always thought spooky old ladies were about the scariest people in the world.

When my father had our cottage built on Lake Leelanau, I was six. It was 1927. Between our cottage and Nedows Bay there were two houses, one of which Al Grogan lived in, and one of which I believe later became the Kuhn Cottage but was then a tea room owned by Mrs. Maro. Other than that, we had deep woods in back and nothing but woods between us and Cemetery Point—about a half-mile north of our cottage on a long spit of beach.

Daddy bought our three-hundred foot lot for $12.00 a front foot. The depth of the lot was the lake back to M-22 one half mile. "Old"

Fred Roth, who sold it to him, was hard up. He offered Daddy all the land he owned from our cottage to Cemetery Point for $5,000 and Daddy couldn't afford it. If he had been able to, we would all now be living on the French Riviera every winter.

In 1982 the land and our cottage were appraised: $1,500 for the cottage, and $89,600 for the land. Long-time Lelander Betsy Holt said once, and I agree, "The land and beach from the Holts to the Lockwoods is the garden spot of Leland." I was grateful to grow up in this garden spot.

The two out-of-work carpenters my father sent up to build the cottage could not get rooms anywhere in Leland because the Leland people were mad at imported help. So I think they stayed at Suttons Bay. The word "carpenter" is too general, "drunken carpenter" is more like it, because one, while drunk, fell off the ladder and broke his leg, end of his help. The other one built on and on and on and on. Our cottage faced south east and was in a lee shore—loved by aquaplaners and water skiers. Daddy cursed them all.

Frank Ake, who worked for my father's company, took up a load of furniture and reported back to my father, "John, I think you'd better get up there right away. The whole house looks awfully queer." Queer was an understatement. The end result of building on and on and on was a dining room that was nine feet too long and no stairway at all to get upstairs. The stairway that happened after that was almost as steep as a ladder. The result of the long dining room (it's the biggest room in the cottage) was two sleeping porches upstairs on the end of the house. I slept on one of the porches, with screens on two sides and open to the weather. I especially liked it on rainy nights. Daddy slept in the big sleeping porch next to my mother's room. Later when we needed more storage space, my sleeping porch was enclosed and had shelves and, of course, fishing equipment and anything else we didn't know where to put. It is a giant closet now called the Fish Room.

A few years ago when I still owned half of the cottage, my sister Babe and I were going over a list of "things that have to be done." She said, "One of the fire dogs is broken. Who can we get to weld it?"

Reply from me, "I'm pretty sure there's a fire dog in the Fish Room."

There was. Every cottage needs a Fish Room. But it was my airy, windswept bedroom as a child.

Of Love and Leland

For years our front yard was just dirt and trees and flagstones from the porch steps to the dock steps. We knew each flagstone by bare feet, and each of us had a favorite one. It was a sad day when Mother, I guess trying to keep up with Mrs. Boozer and Dorothy Appel, had the stones taken away and round pieces of redwood put down instead. (However, that was much later. Now things have come full circle and we couldn't afford flagstones when the wooden things rotted out.) My daughter Kit and her husband Tim fixed that perfectly with cement squares in 1984 as they became the new generation at Leland.

                ා   ා   ා

We always left for Leland right after school let out. We yearned for the lake, especially the cool water. Before we went north, no children I know of were allowed to swim in a swimming pool. Polio was a terrible scourge then. Mother was sure that it came from flies. You can lose your appetite in a hurry when your mother uses a fly swatter right next to your dinner plate. Once and only once she got one of those obscene strips of sticky paper and hung it from the ceiling. Flies are attracted to it and then they get stuck. Presumably we couldn't get polio from those flies anyway. My father put a stop to that the first time he saw it.

Another reason for Leland summers was, of course, that in Indianapolis and everywhere else there was no air-conditioning. 4401 Broadway had no attic and a slate roof that seemed to concentrate the heat. Sometimes we lay all evening in cool water in the bathtubs to try to cool off. And often Daddy took his mattress out to the backyard, once greatly surprising the night watchman for our block, hired after the Lindberg kidnapping. I guess he thought Daddy was a burglar who was taking a nap in his underwear before commencing his night's thieving.

Our early trips to Leland were a blur of excitement. I'm sure they were two days of misery for Mother. The car was loaded to the gunwales with three children, the cook, and Petie, our Airedale. In those days the spare tire was sensibly mounted on the back of the car. This was so convenient that the car makers abandoned it. After twelve hours of hard driving, we reached the Pantlind Hotel in downtown Grand Rapids. Another day like the first got us to "Green Acres," Daddy's name for the cottage. The farther north we drove, the more gravel roads there were. After a few days, Traverse City mover Joe Hahnenberg crashed down the driveway with Mother's wardrobe trunk in his big truck. It was so high we lost branches every time he came down. No matter—our clothes were here. Our wardrobe trunk had four deep drawers, and we each had a drawer for all our clothes for the summer. (We always left plenty of clothes up there over the winter.) It took three strong men to handle the huge trunk up and around corners to the sleeping porch on the second floor of the cottage. Joe used to plead with Mother to bring just suitcases, but she never listened.

Petie was our first family dog. We got her as a puppy and her kennel name was "Rose Bud." Well, none of us could handle that name, so there was a big argument led by me. I was determined that her name be "Nancy Carroll" after my favorite movie star. Daddy thought that was worse than Rose Bud. Finally, to stop all wrangling, Daddy said firmly, "Her name is Petie, and that's that."

Petie didn't just swim after our boat when we went fishing; she swam after any boat she could see. On a calm day we could spot an arrow-shaped ripple with Petie's head at the apex, near a motor cruiser. She never wanted to be taken onboard, just swam around the boat a couple of times, said "Hello" or "Good Luck" and headed for home or another boat.

We all know that dogs can tell time. And, of course, Petie could, too. An elderly couple rented a cottage down from us one summer and took a regular morning walk with Petie as their companion. If they hadn't come by ten-thirty, Petie went and got them.

Neighbor Julie Brooks Cunningham had a beautiful red setter, Skippy. He and Petie were truly bosom pals and soul mates. When we arrived for the summer, Skippy was usually in our driveway or else got there in two minutes from his house, Northfields. As we were driving by Northfields, Mother always gave two long and two short blasts on the horn, "AH-OO-GAH!" If Skippy were in earshot, he arrived in the backyard as we did. It will be hard to believe the greetings between these two dogs. Barking with pure joy, they'd stand on their back legs and hug each other. They acted more like people than people. After a prolonged greeting, they ran off to do some project that Skippy had in mind. Since both dogs had had the services of a veterinarian, their friendship was purely platonic. Petie may have had more fun than any of us. He and Skippy met every morning after breakfast. Petie had the best smile of any dog I've known.

"The Bloody Ghost Tree" was probably our Leland logo. It's in the backwoods near the road. A beech, it goes up about six feet and then goes parallel to the ground and has a snout. Then two trunks go on straight up to make it one of the very tallest trees there. None of us has ever driven to the cottage for the first time in the summer without checking to see how "Bloody" fared during the winter. Daddy named it the first year we were in the cottage, 1927. He fretted each summer because he wanted a picture of it, but the woods had so much shade that no one could take a good picture; that is, no one did till my husband, Frank, started coming to Leland. He earned Daddy's undying gratitude by getting a great portrait of this unusual landmark.

"Green Acres" was also Daddy's idea of a name for the cottage, and was really done facetiously in an argument with Charlotte Smith (Mrs. Francis, from Buffalo). They were really poking fun at some of the pretentious names of the cottages. She retaliated by calling the Smith Cottage, "Island View Heights." After telephones were introduced, our phone messages went like this: "'Island View Heights' calling 'Green Acres.' Are you there, 'Green Acres?'" After the conversation we ended, "'Green Acres,' over and out."

"Green Acres" lacked a few amenities. When I was little we had an icebox. Refrigerators hadn't come along yet, so the ice pick was used to chip off hunks of a fifty-pound block of ice that was delivered each week. There was a pan on the floor underneath it to catch the melted ice. I think the ice was taken from Lake Leelanau when it was frozen, but I'm not quite sure. Then in summer it was in the ice house near the end of the channel covered with sawdust to keep it from melting. All of my own grandchildren would be lucky to chip off a piece of ice to suck as I, Babe and Johnny did. I don't know why it tasted better than ice cubes, but it just did. We never could freeze anything, of course, and there were no frozen foods, so the fresh food that came in the kitchen door was used that day or it spoiled.

We also grew up with a kerosene water heater. The lake supplied water, but it wasn't hot. The heater lived where the toilet now is downstairs in the cottage. I am sure a safety inspector would have swooned with horror had he seen it. I didn't think it was so dangerous, just too hard to light. You had to have three hands to do it. The lighting instructions were tacked on the wall over it, but they got blurred by age and by not being noticed. The only way to light it was to lie on your back with a lighted kitchen match in one hand. With the other hand you pushed a little button, maybe a pilot light, with your third hand you immediately turned the wick to "LOW." Since digital dexterity has never been my long suit, I was told, "Don't go near it." One day though, when no one was home but me, I thought I'd take a nice hot bath. The little room that housed the heater sort of caught on fire. I can't remember really, but I expect that was my last hot bath for the summer. Well, the water wasn't really hot, more like lukewarm. And if Daddy took a hot bath, he used all the hot water and then yelled for minions (my brother Johnny and me) to get him kettles of boiling water to pour in.

There was another antique I never noticed when I was little, but when I was old enough to have dates and go to dances, I noticed it a LOT. The bathroom light! It hung from the ceiling with a very dark shade. This was so situated that if I were trying to put on make-up or fix my hair, I sometimes combed the lamp shade. The medicine chest had a tiny mirror, but even if I peered closely, I just got a shadowy image. I'm not sure how the custom began, but everybody seemed to know I primped in the dark. Maybe someone heard me gripe about it. Anyway, as I came downstairs to my waiting gentleman, he would say, "Gosh, you look so pretty tonight," and then pretend to stifle an explosion of laughter. This scenario got less and less excruciatingly funny.

Frank hated the bathroom light worse than I did, so our first expense when I owned half of the cottage was to get the new fluorescent light in the ceiling.

               ଏଓ   ଏଓ   ଏଓ

My brother Johnny and I used to have to drink boiled milk because it was a pre-pasteurized era. It was unbelievably terrible. Mother never would even taste it. The cook, Cora, knew what it was like, though, and she sneaked it away so we hardly drank any.

We were also subjected to fertile eggs for a while, but not too long, I think. We didn't know about this then, but way back in the hills was Daddy's bootlegger. He took care of the liquid needs during Prohibition. I don't know what he made in his still, corn liquor maybe, but along with the liquor Daddy had to buy eggs from his wife. She was kind of a gypsy spooky dirty-looking person. Fertile eggs do not keep very well and they are always so smelly. We were always served a boiled egg for breakfast. No matter how fresh they were they smelled awful, and once when Johnny or I found a little hunk of blood, or what we decided was a feather, we mutinied for all time.

A well was dug when the cottage was built. We had drunk a lot of well water. Daddy sent a sample of the water to Lansing, Michigan to be tested for purity one August. The report came back after Labor Day when Daddy had already gone home. The gist of the message was that the well "was very badly contaminated," and no one must ever drink one drop of it. Daddy called Dr. Winters, our pediatrician, and the word was sent. Typhoid shots for everyone who had drunk any of the water. My mother had had typhoid fever as a child, and Babe, then an infant, drank only boiled water. So Johnny and I and Mary Cunningham, still with us, were taken to Suttons Bay for a series of three typhoid shots. The second two I can't even remember, probably because all three of us thought we were dying after the first one. Mother had three very sick and prostrate people on her hands with high fever, splitting headaches, and arms swollen to twice their normal size.

A new well was dug and the well water came out of a hand pump on the side of the sink. You'd pump and pump the handle, the pump sort of groaned, gasped and gagged, and then a trickle of brown water came out. So all of us just drank lake water all the time. That's what came out of the faucets anyway. I kind of wondered about that as a child, especially after a man drowned off Warden's Point across the lake and his body was never found. I remember I carefully inspected the filter (so-called) between us and the Appels. It was just a piece of screening, so nothing big like a piece of body, I thought, could come through.

Septic tank and water trouble are the bane of a cottage owner's existence. One year for about a month our next-door neighbors, the Lockwoods, couldn't get enough water pressure, so they tapped into our hose some way or other. I know it ran across our yard and into their house, but Daddy liked it because about every other afternoon Aunt Harris Lockwood would come wailing over, saying "John, please let me take a bath!" Sometimes he would and sometimes he wouldn't. Aunt Harris was eminently teasable, and in those days she was lots of fun.

There had been a bell in the front yard for years. It was a gift from Althea and Julie Brooks (a.k.a. The Brooks Brothers) to Mother and Daddy. They were spinster twins who lived in Northfields. There was a great and hilarious bell-raising party when I was about ten. What was the bell for? It was for "Dinner is on."

Once after Johnny was in a National One sailing regatta, he gave a party. George Ball got a bit too excited and climbed the bellpost, and he was no lightweight. End of post. So the bell was in the pumphouse till 1984 when our new generation put it out again. You can still hear it from a long way off.

The Brooks sisters had a real slot machine in their basement. Great fun on rainy days. How about that for getting rid of kids who are being a nuisance? "Go play the slot machine." We worked it so the grown-ups gave us change, and if we won we kept the money. I expect Althea and Julie unlocked it and took all the quarters to give to us to use on our next visit to their gambling den. No one needs an elaborate game room. Put in a slot machine in your basement. That's all you need.

As we were growing up, Daddy, who loved to fish, rented a very ancient boat which looked as old as Noah's Ark from local fisherman Jake Schwarz every summer. He called it *The Nameless*. It had a cranky engine in the middle of the boat and wooden seats all around, and Daddy was the one who taught us how to fish. We had to bait our own hooks and take off our own fish unless it unfortunately had swallowed the hook. We refused to do the disgorging because the fish's eyes popped out so horribly. We were all supposed to clean them, but we never did.

One of my favorite memories was watching Emily Benedict (Mrs. Horace) and Johnny Jameson try to clean a fish without touching it. They used a stick and pliers and heaven knows what else. Aunt Harris' father, "Pappy Bingham," lived with the Lockwoods and used to pay us children ten cents for twenty-five tiny frogs in a nearby pond. We stopped upon learning that he used them as live bait. Worms, we thought, didn't feel so bad put on a hook, but little frogs—no way.

Of course, there were no telephones anywhere except in Bishop Woodcock's house, which is now Lena Ball's. If you should get a telegram—always dire news—it might come in two or three days. Actually, it was delivered whenever Mr. Ross' son got on his bicycle and rode out to your house with it. Mr. Ross was a combination telegraph-sender and mortician. Mail and Indianapolis papers came three or four days later than they should have, but nobody cared, and days went by when we didn't even go to the post office.

Our cottage was between the Lockwoods and the Appels, and Nancy, Ellie and I were best friends off and on. I do recall an "Ellie Rebellion Club." We never called through the woods to each other, but left notes written on birch bark in a hollow stump about a half a mile in back of

"Green Acres," quite near the Bloody Ghost Tree. All of us used to explore back there because we thought every mound had a dead Indian under it, and we decided early on that an Indian had pulled the Bloody Ghost Tree over to use as a landmark for them. Maybe one did.

The only electricity came from the Falls right by what is now the Cove. Local resident Jake Schwarz was in charge of the power house. I think the power house was either right on the Falls or where the Cove is now. The electricity was so feeble that if it thundered in Canada all the lights in the county went out for two or three days sometimes. But it didn't bother us too much; we had plenty of candles and flashlights, and cooked with propane gas. Jake got to the power house by walking on two boards with no railings over the Falls. A child caught doing this was in big trouble.

The Leland Mercantile did not carry vegetables (it had everything from nails to cakes), so David Couturier, a farmer near Leland, had a big vegetable truck. He came around twice a week to every cottage. Mother was always cross with him because he would never vary his route, and he always went to the Indiana Woods first, so her choice of vegetables was slim. David was a Manitou Market on wheels.

The Merc was a marvelous place. As you went in on the left side there was a soda fountain, and Uncle Ralph Lockwood always treated us. But even better, across the store was one glass counter full of brick hard brown sugar, chunks of it. You would buy a piece, say the size of a half a brick, for about ten cents, and then if you wanted to take a bite, you had to use the ice pick and hammer. You put this rock-hard piece of sugar in your mouth and just sucked the sweetness as it melted gradually. Strange to say, we have our teeth still, and it was probably the best tasting thing of my childhood. Stealing a sibling's brown sugar hunk was a low trick.

There was another grocery store across the street—shabby, run down and owned by the crossest man in Leland. One day Mr. Preston Joyes wanted to buy some lemons. No lemons at Merc. The Merc was, then as now, always out of something. Mr. Joyes crossed the street to the bum little grocery and asked the owner for some lemons. Answer: "Don't order lemons no more. Can't keep 'em in stock. They go too fast."

Ellie Appel and I lived next door to each other. Lutie Schaf was on

"The Big Lake." She later married Alan Appel, Ellie's brother. Ellie had a special afternoon game when we were about eight or nine. It was certainly very simple, but hard to describe because today's route from the cottage to Cemetery Point is blocked by rows of cottages and docks. We walked to Cemetery Point, all forested, no paths in the woods at all. Then we went out on the end of the spit of sand without getting our feet wet. Wet feet meant you lost before the game really got going. We came home "by bank," which meant we scrambled along the bank that led from the level ground down to the lake, usually ten to twenty feet. In a few places there was a two or three foot beach, but mostly not though. If you went up to the level ground, you lost. Most of our travel was by hanging on one tree root after another. Dumb, but fun. It was harder than it sounds on that precipitous shoreline.

About three afternoons a week one summer all three of us had to do what Daddy called "The Channel Swim." Then the Lockwoods were renting next to the Maus in Al Grogan's Cottage. With Daddy in a rowboat beside us, we had to swim to the Lockwood dock. The length of the swim didn't bother us much—probably a quarter of a mile—what was on the bottom of that deep water surely did, though, especially my sister Babe when she was old enough to do "The Channel Swim." As we got about to the site of the present day Capps Cottage (it wasn't there yet), the bottom had all sorts of yucky things: tree trunks, stumps, old branches. We thought there could be almost anything horrible, so we did that part of the swim with our eyes shut, or doing the back stoke, trying to think Alan Appel was a liar. He always said our lake had a monster in it down there like the Loch Ness, and that he had seen it.

In addition to *The Nameless* fishing boat we had two rowboats, one skinny and easy to row. The other was a Maine fisherman's dory sent to Leland (God knows how) by Uncle Booth Tarkington. This one was very unpopular. The oar locks were U-shaped pieces of metal on each side and the oars had to be feathered at every stroke. If we used that boat in a rowboat race, we were always last. "Mother's Lake" wasn't the Atlantic Ocean, nor were we accomplished Maine oarsmen. Each night the boats were pulled up on wooden ramps on either side of the dock.

Never let it be said that my siblings were not ingenious. After a few cottages had been built on our lake front, they decided to give the inhabitants a treat, and incidentally have a ball themselves. They took our rowboat ramps, put a wooden chair on each, and then each of them took the ramp out with a canoe paddle. The ramps were so waterlogged that they were four or five inches under the water. Ergo, an evening vision of two kids paddling on chairs on the lake and having a sprightly conversation. They always conversed and acted, they thought, as if they weren't doing anything unusual at all. The vision should have made people do a double-take, but one or both of them usually fell off thus ending any speculation about twentieth century miracles. Anyway, they had fun.

You will think that our fun was pretty tame, but if you dove under an upside down rowboat and breathed and talked, you were having a lot of fun. Also it was a little scary. This was one of our morning recreations when we were little. Later on it was too boring to bail the boat out afterward, so we quit.

Another project was to see how many cartwheels in a row or at once you could do in the front yard. We were even into backovers, as we used to call them. It was harder than what we call frontovers. We weren't exactly Mary Lou Retton, but so what?

Mary Stuart Socwell (Mrs. Louis Stephanoff, my first cousin), always came up from Indianapolis for a visit and sometimes Jeanette Tarkington (Mrs. Alfred Stokely), and often Mig Jameson (Mrs. William Wildhack). Jeanette, a superior cartwheeler, usually stayed with the Appels; Cousin Mary June Appel was alive then. Alan one year put a live garter snake in Jeanette's bed or down her neck, I forget which, but anyway she moved to our cottage.

The Leland Country Club was founded when I was little. As you can imagine, the golf course was pretty raggedy, but we didn't care. Mother taught all three of us how to play golf; no golf pros in olden times. You learned a sport by yourself or with a patient parent. Professional teachers are part of the Brave New World. She practically dragged us around, as we muttered, "We don't want to learn how to play golf." But learn we did. And we can all play a decent game. The first nine holes in a row that Babe played with Phyllis Cattell, she remembers that she shot 209 and Phyllis shot 183. Once an adult golfer said to Babe, "Are you a golfer?" "No," she said, "I'm a Jameson."

Mr. Ralph Gould taught his four daughters golf, too. Two of them, Maryellen Hadjisky and Lucy Butterbaugh, were always in Leland every summer and they are both very good players. When their father thought they were good enough and knew golf manners, he used to send them up to play by themselves. They picked up score cards, went to the beach, filled them out, and lied through the Goulds' dinner hour about how they played this or that hole.

Right beside the old fourth green and the fifth tee, there's a water fountain put up in memory of Mr. Gould, a dear man. He always said right there, "I sure wish I had a glass of water."

I don't want a fountain as my memorial. I want a tasteful redwood outhouse by the birch grove behind the fourteenth green, maybe with a nice little brass plate, too. That's where I always said, "I sure have to go to the bathroom." I think if people want to give a gift in my memory, just say, "Donations to the Leland Country Club." Just think of the grateful ladies!

We were ensconced in June. My father always arrived the first day of August for a month. His routine never varied. He always went straight to the bar for a drink, put on his fishing hat, sat in the rocker on the porch, and said, "Well, it's the first day of summer." One year he wrote that he'd give a silver dollar to the first child who yelled, "Fancy meeting you in Leland," as he drove down the driveway. Mary Stuart, Johnny and I literally spent the day in the backyard waiting for him. I think we yelled in unison. We never had the slightest idea that he had a silver dollar for each of us. Once I guess he was pretty bored with Mary Stuart's and my noisy activities, and he offered us (remember inflation was down then), twenty-five cents to walk from our house through the Indiana Woods and back of the Elder Blackledge's, and climb the fire tower. We did. He had an uninterrupted nap and we had blisters and a quarter.

    Daddy thought he was the boss, and we let him think so, except about 8:45 every morning. Breakfast was at 9:00 AM sharp. His three children lay on their beds already dressed until he began to wake up. You did not get up until the *pater familias* did. My father did not wake up quietly or quickly. Rumble of his bedsprings, then "Oh me, oh me, oh me," louder and louder. Then came "Lordy, Lordy, Lordy." The last "Lordy" was our signal. As he wandered into the hall with his chamber pot and Brooks Brothers nightshirt with initials on the pocket yet, we jumped out of bed, all three of us. We dashed into the bathroom and shut and locked the door. It took us no time at all to brush our teeth, go to the bathroom and come out ready for breakfast. The bathroom was quite crowded, but we had a system. We had to beat him in because he took about an hour to get ready for breakfast. Daddy was always predictable in the morning. As he waited for his ungrateful young, it was "Judas Priest. You damn little birds," then "So help me, Mrs. Eddy," and the last shout "I outrank you, dammit."

    All three of us always left lights on, only I was the worst offender, and you could have heard his bellow for miles. "LIGHTS, DAMMIT!" Daddy always claimed he spent more money for three months in Leland than nine months in Indianapolis. I believe it. High utilities were one of the joys of country living.

☙ ☙ ☙

I think some of the pleasures of our childhood were different from those at Leland today. I may be wrong on this, but our parent's generations and ours seemed to do a lot more together. I can prove this with some old snapshots of our dock around noon on a nice day. Conservatively speaking, it was jammed with grandparents, parents, three dogs, five or six or more kids, and always a couple of boats tied up. The adults had their elevenses, the kids were swimming in and out of the boats, and senior citizens had a bench and everyone had a great time!

One day at noon as we were playing around with the aquaplane on our dock, Mr. and Mrs. John Norton appeared in their bathing suits to visit our parents. They were Proper Bostonians, and he was silent and somewhat dour, we thought. They lived in one of those rich houses south of the Fish Docks. He put his drink down and beckoned me to come into the dock with the boat. I did. Then he held onto the aquaplane and said, "Gun it." I gunned it and he stood on his hands for a few turns around to great applause from the dock. Then he climbed back on the dock without talking and resumed drinking his drink. My Gosh! We'd never even seen him swimming.

Johnny swears that one day he was on the dock and looked towards Cemetery Point. There was our father sitting on a chair on this aquaplane, towed behind a slowly moving boat. The logistics of this maneuver escape me, but I believe it.

Johnny Jameson actually said to me a year or so ago, "Our parents led such restricted lives, always going to the same place for the summer." That's BALONEY! They were luckier than most people in the world. THEY HAD A BALL. I suppose the "restricted lives" bit comes from a comparison with the Cottinghams, our relatives, who dropped in and out of Leland on their way to Budapest or some other exotic spot. Our parents didn't want to travel. They had Leland and lots of gaiety. I remember how much they laughed. Cousin Fred Appel used to say, "Florence Jameson is the prettiest girl in Leland." Yes, when Mother was having fun, she sparkled. And no, I am not implying anything about my mother's morals. One wonders, though, about summer friendships. The husbands were often gone—was there more than the usual temptation? After her death we went through her things. There was a letter in a box in the back corner of her closet shelf from a Leland gentleman. The salutation was, "My Darling." Was it a fond salutation from a friend?

My father and mother had different interests, it is true. In Indianapolis my mother could just barely get my father to go once a week to play bridge with their friends. His knee-jerk response to any invitation was "No." She loved parties and he professed to hate them, but in Leland he shed worries and was very social, social for him that is. He seemed so much younger in Michigan.

Once a summer there was a party that did not include children, Althea and Julie's "Kitchen Party," called this because the first one was given in the cavernous kitchen of Northfields. It got more and more elaborate. One year the Kitchen Party was a fancy dress ball at the Country Club. I remember that Daddy dressed as a Princeton undergraduate and Mother as a flapper. They didn't rent their costumes: they had their costumes, all but Daddy's mustache, which he made with Petie's hair and adhesive tape. He even had a boater (a stiff straw hat).

Bill Dabney, from Louisville, whose parents had a cottage during the summer, and I made plans to spy on the party. We rendezvoused at our dock after dark to row to the Nedows Bay. There are no more eager voyeurs than kids spying on their parents. Although we were far from the revelers, we whispered. I hissed, "Do you think we should muffle the oars?"

Turning into Ashley Wilkes, Bill whispered back, "Ah will avert ma eyes, Ma'am, so you can tear up yo' petticoats."

We were so charmed with our raillery that it took some time and a lot of giggles to get started rowing (without petticoats).

We did make it to the dock in Nedows Bay, down a steep hill from the country club, and climbed the hill. We planned to crawl up to the long windows and lie on our stomachs to look in. Our resolve was threatened when we thought we heard someone or some two in the bushes back of the white bench.

We only peeked a few minutes, but saw enough. Singing, dancing, kissing and drinking. In other words, one helluva party! Bill and I didn't discuss what we were thinking. The rules parents gave us, and they did this! "It was a puzzlement," to paraphrase the King of Siam.

We crept back to the boat avoiding the bushes. We rowed home silently; nor did we ever talk to each other or anyone else about our evening.

The Jameson dock was sparsely populated the next noon. Bill did stroll down though, and said to me, "Good Mahnin, Miss Scarlett, Ah hope you slept well aftah our strenuous evenin." I forget what I said.

Johnny, Babe, I, and probably everyone else in Leelanau County who is old enough remembers the two weeks of the Dining Room Table. The Tarkingtons had sent it to us. It was painted dull black with roses on the leaves and curved legs—absolutely hideous! Finally Mother could not stand it any longer, so we started sanding and scraping. Daddy had gone home and the September weather was frightful, but Dr. Winters hadn't given the OK (no polio) to come home message. The cottage was filled with kids of all ages, all of whom got handed sandpaper. No mechanical sanding in olden times; lots of elbow grease though. When it was down to the bare wood, it was a beautiful mahogany, and Johnny Jameson, who could equal anybody in refinishing, did a stunning job. It's an oil finish. He even did something which was new in those days. He put a finish on it that wouldn't get circles from water marks. If you can imagine the wind howling and rain pouring and about a dozen kids at once working, eating and giggling and listening to the Victrola, you would remember it as a banner week. Mother rustled sandwiches and changed the records on the Victrola, I think, and "plumped" the pillows. And she probably lugged in wood as well. Her idea of fun was to have people at the cottage, but she also wanted a house to look ready for company, the more the better. My brother Johnny wrote a postcard one year to his grade school sweetheart. Of course, we all read it.

Dear Ann,

I'm having a nice time. Mother keeps the house real neat.

After Frank came to Leland, starting in 1945, the first sign of getting up time for Frank and me were two noises: one, Mother winding the clock, and two, "plumping up" the pillows. In fact, concerning "plumping," he forbade me to do it, and as for the clock, we let it run down and never wound it. After she died, we had half the cottage, but her presence and that of my father lingered. These old cottages are as full of memories as a spring boathouse is full of spiderwebs.

There were two kinds of picnics when we were teenagers, one with our own age friends and those with parents and their friends and others. The first kind weren't terribly much fun, sandy hot dogs and warm beer, and someone always forgot to bring something vital like mustard or buns. Hank Holt, from Indianapolis, and I happily solved this problem by having our dinner at our own houses and then going to the beach party. We could tell pretty much what was going on even before we reached the fire. Most couples were sitting together facing the fire; also there were at least two pairs of legs, sometimes four, somewhat entangled. The owners of these legs were lost in the darkness. Well, beaches can have aphrodisiac qualities, but the people I'm thinking about didn't need a lot of extra stimulation. They still go to Leland and are grandparents.

And now we come to PERFECT PICNICS. The perfect picnic was orchestrated by Horace Benedict, Mary Anthony's father, and Charlotte Smith's brother, "Ben," as we called him. He was a picnic genius!

He could even order perfect weather. He worked all day, carrying beach chairs, getting firewood, chilling martinis, getting beautiful steaks, and lots more. Charlotte made a gigantic pot of coffee ahead of time, and we just had to warm it. None of this warm water, coffee grounds and egg shells. Someone always made German potato salad. Mother sliced about a dozen onions and simmered them in two sticks of butter all day as sauce for the steaks. Then we drove to one of several picnic sites, all far from civilization. Charlotte always voted for what she named "The Hideaway." The path down to the beach was right across from today's "Happy Hour." We went down a rutted road which turned into a path. Now it's paved and has cottages on each side. On M-22 there were three places, all uninhabited then, the "Sunken Cabin," the "Springs," and "Bob's Park." Our daughter Susie went to her first picnic when she was two years old. The first thing she did was to sit in a little stream that flowed out of the woods to the lake and drink some of the water. I said to Dr. Capps, "I suppose the water is safe."

Answer: "I wouldn't think so. Some gypsies who camped back in the woods got typhoid last month." Then casually, "I wouldn't worry, it's too late now anyway."

I did not feel so casual.

At one picnic Daddy had to carry Aunt Harris down to the beach. She had slipped on our porch steps and broken her ankle. So she insisted Daddy carry her because it was all his fault that she fell. That was a sight! He needed CPR long before he reached the beach and got some helpers to carry her. She really did slip and it was his fault, too.

Painting the porch steps each August was Daddy's ritual act as a cottage owner. He never put up a wet paint sign. After the painting, we'd sit on the porch and see who would be the first one to mar the wet paint. It was usually Petie, and no, we never fixed the paw marks. Daddy didn't expect poor Aunt Harris.

I hope no one ever takes off the door handle from the porch side of the front door of the old cottage. It has Petie's teeth marks on it. Petie slept on the porch couch. He was terrified of storms and tried to bite his way into the house if he thought we took too long to rescue him. It never took very long. Between bites on the door handle, he wailed like a Banshee.

At PERFECT PICNICS there was usually swimming, drinks for the grown-ups, and a meal fit for the gods. The last part of these picnics was always my favorite. We sang and watched the sun set over North Manitou. Someone always brought a harmonica, and if not, we sang anyway. The last song was always "Hi, Lili, Hi, Lo." Sound corny? You bet! In my declining years one of my projects will be to mount a crusade to make "corny" a good adjective instead of a pejorative one. In my lexicon it will mean "memorable," "great fun," "repeated annually, at least," and edging up to PERFECT.

"Sticky Stones." These were a very potent Leland totem for anyone who was originally a Smith or Jameson and all of their sisters, brothers, cousins, aunts, spouses, children and grandchildren. Johnny and Sally Smith discovered them, and I think Charlotte, her mother, named them. Instructions follow herewith: Pick up a little white pebble on Big Beach near the water's edge, but not wet. Put it on your lip. If it sticks, it's a sticky stone. If it falls off, you just keep on trying, that is, if you want to. Do not wet your lips. It has powers to amuse—or console.

I have a small supply here at home for emergencies. During our daughter Susie's freshman year at Smith she met her future husband, Jack Mead, during Christmas vacation. When I took her to the airport to go back to school, there was Jack in the airport. He'd put his sister Edie on a plane, but just happened to be wandering around near the gate Susie was departing from. I don't think I have seldom, if ever, seen Susie lose her cool, but she came close that morning. She greeted Jack and I think we chatted a few minutes. I was about to kiss her goodbye and leave them. Suddenly Susie turned from both of us and fled for the shelter of the airplane. Naturally, I sped home and sent her a sticky stone and a copy of A.E. Houseman's poem that begins, "When I was one and twenty. . . ."

               ఌ   ఌ   ఌ

Ever since my brother Johnny had seen his first sailboat he had been yearning and begging for one. I think that's where a family saying was coined. Every time he asked for a sailboat my father would say, "I want a pony." This meant "end of discussion." When he was ten or eleven, Johnny was at a farm in Illinois and fell out of a tree, breaking his elbow very badly. It had to be rebroken and reset after my parents rushed over to get him. Of course, after weeks in a cast, he had to undergo very painful physical therapy. As usual that summer, we all went to Leland. Johnny's arm looked like a bent, shriveled stick. But there at the dock was a secondhand Snipe. Johnny had gotten his "pony." A

Snipe is small and easily handled by one person, but you cannot sail it with only one arm. Result: Johnny's arm was straightened out and firm and tanned by the end of the summer. There were no flies on Daddy!

Of course, later on he wanted a BIGGER sailboat. Then came the busy and happy years of the *Two Jay,* a National One design. Wood then, of course. My gentle brother turned into Captain Bligh when we were in the *Two Jay.* By then there was also a Yacht Club and two races a week. I was the regular crew with Johnny, and Babe was needed if there were a lot of wind. Johnny and I sailed over to the Yacht Club and another family saying was born. As Johnny cast off he'd call back to Babe, "Hold yourself in readiness at the dock."

Mother was not thrilled to have her youngest lying on the bow in a heavy wind. She did insist Babe have a bright red life jacket on so she could identify her.

There were about twenty Nationals. Babe and I didn't just sail in races. Almost every damn day we rigged the boat and sailed with Johnny, practicing jibes and speedy come-abouts. In a race, Johnny never said, "Prepare to come-about." He just shouted "Ready about. Hard-A-Lee." We could have turned the *Two Jay* around on a dime. I could get the jib trimmed almost before he finished yelling. I expect all this practice plus sanding the bottom of the hull before every race may have played some part in the plaques in the Yacht Club. Johnny was a true genius at light-weather sailing. The other sailors complained that he could smell a bit of wind where there was a flat calm.

Once Babe and Johnny were sailing in a very light wind. He reached over and pulled a few strands of hair from her head and threw them into the water to see how fast he was going. He may not remember it. Babe does! Why didn't he pull out his own hair?

One June before the racing season began, Captain Bligh decided we would hoist up the *Two Jay* at Jake Schwarz's boat house near where the library is now. I used the word "we" incorrectly. Babe and I would sand and paint the boat under his supervision. I was sanding in a slot next to Jean Gilligan, Jack's twin. We had to lie on our backs on some kind of raft as we sanded and painted. This meant your back was sopping wet and you had grit and paint all over your front. One day Jack was taking a tour of duty. He called to me as I was taking a rest and said, "Do me a favor, Susie, go ask Jake for a sky hook and a left-handed monkey wrench."

Always obliging, I said, "OK."

I found Jake and asked him. Jack had crept up behind me and he and Jake bent over double howling with laughter. I still don't know why my mistake was all that hilarious. How was I supposed to know? But I was never allowed to forget it. That whole summer every time I ran into Jake he'd look at me and start laughing all over again, or he might say in a voice you could hear for blocks, "Susie, come on over, I just got some sky hooks in."

When Johnny went overseas in World War II, Babe and I decided to race the *Two Jay* in one of the informal races. The hardest part was always milling around in Nedows Bay jockeying so as to be ON the starting line when the gun went off and also to be the windward boat. Babe was the captain, and just at the worst of the milling around she dropped the sheet and tiller, and said, "You have to do it. You're the oldest." We were first around the Sunken Island buoy and then we didn't know what to do. I thought we should be on a reach and Babe thought wing and wing. So we just luffed till the next boat came around and we copied it. The other boat won. Johnny would not have liked that.

Before the war, Mother, Charlotte Smith and Mrs. Workum were the judges at every race. They were very, very good and their word was law. They did lots of drilling, too. I can't imagine three ladies who enjoyed themselves more two afternoons a week.

One year, there was a big National regatta, probably about forty boats. This was the final race. There was a howling north wind. The boats were flying to the finish line, all wing and wing, when guess who came out in a small outboard loaded to the gunwales with little children? Jim Henning, that's who who has temporarily lost his mind. He stops the boat right spang on the finish line (between the Derricks' dock and the Yacht Club dock). Small children in his boat spot Aunt Greenie, Mrs. Charles Schaf from Indianapolis, who is helping the judges, and they wave and wave and call in piping little voices, "Hello, Mrs. Schaf. Hello, Mrs. Schaf." All the judges are swearing and making wild arm motions which meant, "Get out of the way and NOW." Kiddies just think all those nice people are really waving at us. I don't know the end of the story. I never heard it. I assume Jim got his engine started, or if not, the north wind pushed the captain of the *Pinafore* and his merry little people onto the Nedows Bay beach away from the finish line.

My father used to get so wrapped up with sailing that he didn't take a nap on race days. He either went about by boat to each buoy or drove the car as close as he could get to it. We housed visiting yachtsmen one summer during a big regatta; once a couple and their son stayed with us. Mother heard the little boy say to his parents, "I wonder when they are going to finish their cottage."

❧ ❧ ❧

Love blossomed at Leland as we all grew up. My sweethearts and I had "our song," either "Harbor Lights," or any of the Big Band songs. Babe and her swain liked "Three Salted Peanuts," which, according to our father, they played nineteen times in succession one night when he was trying to go to sleep.

My father was always looking out for his daughters' virtues. Once Babe and her beau returned in the garbage truck he was driving for his summer job. He dropped Babe at the door and left. Daddy heard the truck crash down the hill in back. Then he went back to sleep for about three hours, although he didn't realize it. Then he woke up and, forgetting to see if Babe was asleep in her bed, which she was, grabbing a poker and flashlight, he went cursing around, sweeping through the bushes and woods, expecting to find his ravished child. Unfortunately for my father, Mother and I heard him. We laughed so hard at the breakfast table that he got absolutely livid. He pushed his plate away and stalked down to the dock to go fishing ALONE.

Every summer we received almost daily letters from Uncle Booth—at least I did. He urged me to beg, lie or steal—anything to send him Babe's letters from her swain. But I didn't have much luck.

Charlotte Smith was also on the lookout for her daughters' virtue. It never worked. Charlotte, when curfew time had come and gone, used to take a cane and her flashlight and walk along the bushes on that little dirt road in front of the Smith Cottage calling, "Hoo, Hoo, Sally, Julia." They and their dates always tricked her, either by crouching way down into the bushes or going right through them tearing back to the porch of the cottage and greeting Charlotte demurely, if slightly out of breath.

❧ ❧ ❧

Many in Leland could have given the impression in the thirties and later that they were quite spiritual. Every Saturday night at 7:30 we went to choir practice. Spirituality? Forget it. That was where everyone made evening get-together arrangements. One other good thing did happen though. We learned the "Brother James Air," the one set to the 23rd Psalm. Johnny chose it to be played for our father's funeral and now we all cry when we hear it.

Of course, the Sunday Night Sing was another place to find a date. All the girls sat on the porch tables and swung their legs.

Our teenage evenings were pretty much like teenagers' today, although some of the activities may have changed. If there were no picnic and no parent willing to have a "brawl"—pick one house, everybody go to it, play music loudly, eat and drink, have fun, and leave the house in a mess—we went to the Blue Bird. In our day the Blue Bird was much smaller. The wing by the channel hadn't been built. There were no tables, just booths and a nickelodeon which was played constantly. There was always a skinny little boy asleep in a booth surrounded by comic books. Can't guess?—Jimmy Telgard, the present owner. One night a week we didn't dance at all, we watched. It was the Lelanders' Polka Night. They had a little band and wow! The whole building shook. A fast polka makes jitterbugging look like a minuet. It was great fun to watch them. Local revelers Rita and Pete Carlson were the best dancers, and they never missed one of those evenings.

One summer when Mig Wildhack, one of my first cousins, was visiting us, the Behringers, parents of Jack and Phyllis (Mrs. John H. Holliday) were renting the Fleming Cottage next to the Capps, but that cottage hadn't been built yet. Tom Young was visiting them. He was the only son of Evie Denny's aunt, Mrs. William Young. Tom was a wild man. Instead of sleeping in the cottage, he had a tent a little ways in the woods. Mig and I, being in the neighborhood one day, decided to look inside Tom's tent. We did not expect him to be at home. We were talking outside the tent when with a roar of fury he rushed out and began to shoot at us with a real gun and real bullets. We knew that he had guns with his mother's permission. In fact, Mrs. Young would let Tom have anything he wanted. He probably wasn't shooting to kill us, but we did not wait to find out. We ran for our lives, literally. Tom joined the Royal Canadian Air Force before we were in the war and was shot down, a young eccentric gone before the time when he could have mellowed out.

One summer when Mig and I were in our teens, she visited us in Leland and she and Jack Gilligan (of Cincinnati, later the governor of Ohio) became interested in each other. The last night of her visit they sat on the screened porch on the front of the house and talked for hours. They were not aware that for one thing my father was an inveterate eavesdropper, and for another his sleeping porch was about fifteen feet away from them and had screens on two sides.

After Mig left, Daddy lay in waiting for Jack. The next time he saw him, he smiled wickedly, "You have compromised my niece, and you owe me five thousand dollars." They never saw each other without a reference by Mig's uncle to the $5,000. I think Daddy even threatened to go public with a letter to *The Leelanau Enterprise*, the weekly newspaper. Jack did write a check finally. It's still uncashed.

After Daddy's death in June 1963, Jack wrote to me. Here are parts of his lovely and compassionate letter.

Speaking of Leland, he wrote:

> *What a blessed place and filled with blessed memories reaching back over a quarter of a century. And most of them revolve about the Jamesons in one way or another...*
>
> *One reason I have wanted my children to know Leland is that it is for me a living proof of the existence of God. He who has created such beauty will surely preserve it, enrich and ennoble it... and we will surely one day enjoy an endless Leland with all our old and cherished friends...*
>
> *I know I shall see your father again because I still owe him five thousand dollars. Until then our prayer is that he rest in peace and you find some comfort in the love we bear you.*
>
> *Jack*

When I was about fifteen or sixteen, Daddy bought a secondhand Chris-Craft. It didn't go very fast and had a few scars, but many strictures for us. He had to be in the boat if we used it, and NO ONE went out without his permission. Only he never gave his permission. *The Nameless* had finally gone to her reward. Jake said no one would rent her. I expect Daddy bought the new boat so he could follow the sailboat races.

One very windy day, Jack Gilligan came over after lunch. Daddy went up for his nap. As we wondered what to do with this beautiful day, I had a good idea, "Let's take out the boat."

Jack, wiser than I, was very reluctant. "Your father will kill us."

Airily I said not to worry, he would never even know. Of course, he was persuaded and we had a beautiful afternoon, roaring around in the big waves that threatened to tear out the hull. When we decided it was about time for Daddy to wake up, we headed for home. As we approached the dock, I looked up and there he was standing by the hemlock tree, hands on his hips, lightning playing around his head. In my terrible agitation, instead of turning the throttle down, I turned it to "Full Speed," and we tore right through the dock. I will spare you the account of the rest of the day. It's a memory I seem to have blocked out. When Jack was the governor of Ohio, I asked him once what was the scariest thing about his job. A prompt answer, "Fear of a prison riot." But he added, "There is one thing I do know, I'll never be as scared as I was the day we tore up your father's dock."

Babe was about ten when I and my friends were having such fun and thinking our world would never change. She remembers that she and Jack Gilligan arranged to be married and live in a tree house in our back woods. She is vague about who proposed to whom. She probably checked out some trees as future residences though. The market for tree houses wasn't thriving, so they could have had their pick except, of course, for the "Bloody Ghost."

☙　　　☙　　　☙

If a boy wanted real privacy, he took his lady out in a boat. There wasn't much car driving because wise parents usually said "No." Once a young man had a certain kind of privacy in mind for me. And I didn't know how to get out of it. He'd asked me to go to the club dance with him. If I'd said no, I couldn't very well go with another boy, because he'd asked me about two weeks before the dance.

He came to our dock in his boat, helped me into it with his sweaty hand. Then he skipped gracefully across the bow to get in himself. That is, he tried to skip gracefully, but he slipped and fell in the lake. It was all his fault—who runs around a deck with hard-soled shoes? I had asked if anyone could help me out of this date, and especially the "privacy" part coming home in the boat.

My imminent departure had not gone unobserved. Suddenly there was Bill Dabney, my savior. He could always get a car. He was very definite. He would drive my young date home to get dry clothes, and then all three of us would go to the dance together. The date, he said firmly, could get his boat in the morning. I still had to endure the dance, but every boy there knew to "cut in on the girl who was stuck."

There were always a lot of stags at these Leland dances; i.e., boys who came alone. They could be a very pleasant help in trouble by cutting in and dancing with a girl. Next explanation: we danced cheek to cheek instead of facing each other as dancers do today. In cheek to cheek, as you danced by the stag line, you could, of course, send out a May Day signal without your partner seeing your face or crossed eyes, or lip signals or maybe just a look of desperation. If a girl wanted to really be popular with the stags at our dances, she learned what I can only call "The Cincinnati Fox Trot" very quickly. Stags were not always 100 percent reliable. If the girl were signaling for help, the boy might smile sweetly and cut in on someone else.

There was the ever-present threat to all Leland summer girls that a really cute girl would arrive with her parents for vacation—usually two or three weeks. Babe has said that she and her friends froze out these unfortunate girls, but she did not elaborate a great deal. My age group tried to do this, too, but with very little success, especially when a girl arrived who was very pretty (dumb though) and she resembled Dolly Parton in the most obvious ways, or rather two ways. Her IQ was not important.

One summer there was a big event. For Indianapolis Bill Elder's birthday, his mother rented the mail boat to take some of us to North

Manitou for a picnic. Each girl brought a picnic for herself and her date. My date was Jack Gilligan. Now if I hadn't been about tenth choice and asked at the last minute he would have had a nice picnic supper. Remember that there were no phones yet, so I didn't have any time to make a picnic. Mother and Daddy were having a fancy party—well fancy for Leland—and Mom had put cucumber sandwiches in the icebox under a damp towel. I took some and grabbed some beer or soft drinks. Jack and I had an argument brought on by the Dolly Parton girl and her equally-endowed little sister, when he saw these girls and his friends eating their fried chicken and potato salad while he nibbled on tiny open-faced cucumber sandwiches. On the way home in the darkness there was considerable romantic activity, but not by me. I didn't have the nerve to shove him overboard, so I pretended to go to sleep, not what he had in mind. Back at the cottage he was naturally ravenous, so we got out the leftover turkey and there was lots of it.

If Bill Elder hadn't had this party when he did, there would never have been one at all. The mothers of Leland would have forbidden any future venturing on the unpredictable waves of the Manitou Straits. The next week fisherman Pete Carlson and his father were fishing when their boat caught fire. No life jackets were aboard and no other fishermen saw the fire. Pete held his father up until he was swept into the strong and very cold current around the north end of North Manitou. Then he lost him. Rita, Pete's wife and Susie's birthday cake maker, spent twenty-four hours on the breakwater. Pete, I think, barely recovered himself. He had pneumonia and both of his ears were permanently damaged.

છે   છે   છે

There were two real dances a week with an orchestra from Traverse: one at the country club and one at Northport Point. The Leland girls thought the Northport girls were snooty—and they were. They acted as if Leland girls were real hicks. We were asked to wear long dresses to the Northport dances, but we never did. If we weren't hicks, we were certainly impolite. The same cutting-in rules applied for us Leland girls at Northport as they did in Leland.

Today it scares me even to think of some of those drives back to Leland after the dances. The drivers liked to race two abreast on that curvy road. We must have had charmed lives. Once my date, Jack Behringer, missed a curve and landed us in the Sand Cut. And yes, nearly all the boys had liquid refreshments in their cars. Some things at the club never change. We were vaguely chaperoned by grownups who had come for supper, but if they noticed boys leaving for awhile they didn't do anything about it.

Was I scared on those suicidal drives from Northport? Heavens no. Not a single bit. I think we all felt we were invincible, and that nothing would ever touch us. Probably every young generation feels this way without articulating it. I crossed some sort of a bar, though, when I had children.

It is interesting how lives in Leland crossed in later life. When Babe was on Indianapolis' St. Paul's Episcopal Church Vestry, there was a large church dinner with place cards. Someone checked out the seating and said to Babe, "Oh, poor you, you're next to the Bishop. What will you talk about?" When Babe was introduced to him, instead of giving him the extra courtesy as was his due as the bishop, she cried, "Little Teddy Jones from Northport. You are the only person from Northport who danced with me." "Little" Teddy and Babe found lots to talk about.

Jack was going to get even with me for the cucumber sandwiches. He had a house guest later that summer. I had a date with Jack for a Northport dance. Jack started casually enough, "How did you like Jim? I'm worried about his being here after the trouble back home." I did ask what the trouble had been.

"Well, he got kicked out of the Cincinnati Country Club. Something about coming on too strong with the daughter of one of the board of directors. It was bad, but it was hushed up."

"That's too bad," and that was all I said. My guardian angel was with me that night. Jim was hiding on the floor of the back seat and I just said as he crawled out, "Hi, Jim, try to stay away from cucumbers and country club scandals."

In my teens I was mad for two boys who never looked at me. One was Dane Prugh, a Greek God from East Leland. And I was not the only girl who was smitten. Dane, though, only had eyes for Edie Bruce (Mrs. Charles Hazard). Once during the annual Leland-Northport golf match, Dane's fan club of giggling girls watched him tee off on the first tee. His drive went fifty feet to the left. Poor boy. No wonder.

My other crush was on Jimmy Watkins, John's oldest brother—an older man. He was a junior at Princeton. I was partly mad for him because he was such a good dancer, or so I thought just by watching him with the other girls. He never danced with me—not until he had a houseparty one summer. One of his friends cut in and then he did, too. I floated in bliss. But our dancing days were coming to an end. Everything would change—overnight. We were "crossing the bar" in our own way.

In the summer of 1941, I was reporting to Uncle Booth all the details I knew about my sister's summer romance. She was fifteen years old and having her first experience with a Grand Passion. We didn't *exactly* open his letters or hers to him.

Please secure for me the total correspondence in this case. I should like to publish it with only a slight editing. Do not let any sisterly or even human scruples stand in your way. Remember, within a matter of weeks the principals won't even know what it was all about. (How fitful and flitterbird is the school-age heart!) I remember a dreadful period in my own experience when I was like that (after a summer at Maxinkuckee) through the whole month of September, an object of commiseration by everybody in our neighborhood.

Florence had always been a biddable child, eager to please. I started my campaign to get the letters with considerable optimism. Ignoring any pangs of conscience, I began to mention the letters in conversations. "I bet Uncle Booth would just love to read your letters. He certainly would appreciate it if you'd send them to him," I would say brightly. "He might even send you a present he'd be so glad." This infantile approach might have worked a few years earlier, but not any more! She never even heard me. Smiling vaguely, she wandered away. And all the time Uncle Booth was sending me urgent letters like this one:

I cannot but feel you haven't gone about this correspondence with energy and ingenuity. For instance, I don't believe you've tried so simple a device as "Oh-look-at-that-Giant-across-the street," and when she looks, grab the letters and run. It seems to me that a more active mind would long since have thought of this.

I was in a terrible spot. I could not nerve myself up to outright theft, but everything else I had tried had ended in failure because she seemed dreamily unaware that I even wanted the letters. When she was home, which was not often, she was in another world, one that was impenetrable to my suggestions. Finally, I took a mean and bullying advantage of her bemused condition. Speaking loudly and slowly, I told her she had to let me send those letters to Uncle Booth. I promised that I would not read them, that she would get them back, and that the young man would never know about it. "Well, all right," she said mildly. "You don't have to yell at me."

Uncle Booth was overjoyed and answered immediately after receiving the package of letters:

So far my examination of the files has revealed only the usual stigmata, so much so, that when I read the mss. at the lunch table, your Aunt Susanah would not believe in the genuineness of the missives, but insisted that I had written them myself, as material for a new study of adolescence. However, though incredible to the inexperienced, the symptoms include all the registered phenomena. Strongly marked is the delusion that the subject is writing letters whereas he, of course, mistakes the merely autobiographical for the epistolary and, in addition, records only what he feels most creditable to himself. Note the items of his adventurous peeking in to a saloon maybe going to be raided by the State Police, (proprietors often spread such rumors among their most impecunious visitors who are of the credulous ages.) Note, too, his dark account of being interviewed by the police about firecrackers—how he seeks to put about himself the haunting aura of danger. Also of persecution. Observe symptoms of stuttering when he writes of his viley spiteful parents—how they un-understand him so viciously that he almost decided to end-it-all and get the hell out of there. All of this is typical—I might say pricelessly so—and the subject's ruthless "Old Codger" and "Old Lady," no doubt tottering into their forties, probably ought to remem-

ber when they were 13 to 16 and wanted automobiles, lunch passes and other Rights of the Underprivileged.

Anyhow, this whole household enjoyed every word and gratitude to you is extreme. Now if we could only get hold of Flora's own autobiographical sketches—but I suppose that's too much to hope, and your Aunt Susanah would insist I could write them myself. Not quite—there are some modern touches I wouldn't be up to.

It was bad enough that I had taken advantage of Babe's lovelorn condition. Worse still, was my shameless delight when I read that I, not Babe, was to be rewarded for it. His letter ended, "So pleased was I with your strong arm work that I climbed the rope into the attic, and when I'd combed off my cobwebs, there were you, all fixed to receive six Hitchcock chairs, four yellow ones for the sides and two black for the foot and head of table." (I have done all the work on this book sitting in one of the Hitchcocks.)

Leland was kind of a Never-Never Land. Time seemed endless, probably because we were young and believed that Labor Day would never come. One reason was that we were so far behind on the news. As I have said, there was one telephone in Leland and television hadn't been invented. We certainly didn't need or miss them, and the radio reception was almost nil because radio (NBC) didn't come to the Grand Traverse region until the next year. As a matter of fact, when the Nazis marched into Poland September 1, 1939, I will tell you how we found out about it thirty-six hours later. We had heard some rumors, but then the newspapers were usually three days late. Mr. William Dabney took his car which had a radio, to right behind the old ninth green, the one you used to shoot up by the lake. If he turned his car in a certain direction he could barely hear the news above the static, and that is how we learned that World War II had begun in Europe.

In 1941 I was a senior at Smith College in Northampton, Massachusetts, seven miles from Amherst College. One Sunday I had a blind date with a recent Amherst graduate who was stationed at the Brooklyn Navy Yard. So we spent most of the day at his fraternity house. We were both bored with each other, and he suggested a walk. I said, "Fine. I've always wanted to see Emily Dickinson's grave."

Composing his face into lines of sadness, he said, "I'm sorry. Was she a close relative?"

"Sort of," I answered.

So, while Pearl Harbor was being bombed, I was in a cemetery at Amherst, Massachusetts.

When we went back to the fraternity house, everyone was listening to the news about Pearl Harbor. My date did not stop to say goodbye, but started for the Brooklyn Navy Yard. He was so excited!

He and I corresponded erratically. In his last letter he wrote that he had just been assigned to the cruiser *USS Indianapolis*. After the news of that tragedy was made public, I could only hope that he had died quickly.

December 8 we went to a history lecture by Dr. Hans Kohn, the famous Czechoslovakian born historian, whose works are internationally known. I can still see him clearly fifty odd years later. A couple of times that day he broke into his native tongue. Part of the time he was fighting tears and part of the time his tears were unchecked. He told us young women what we could expect—months and years of war. "You will lose brothers, sweethearts, and husbands. And you will also lose your youth." This was my first inkling of what lay ahead.

The United States was fighting for its life and everyone knew it, against terrible, brutal evil. We did not dare lose this war. We were fighting the Germans who were ready to invade England. If England fell—God help us. Winston Churchill said, "Without victory, we have no chance of survival." Another word which might be cliché now is "Pride," but we very well knew what it meant. There have been histories written about the causes, battles, results, losses, and victories of our war, and it truly was our war. But no one has written about the wives, mothers, sweethearts, widows, and sisters of World War II. We outnumber all the "protesters" put together, and we never protested because we were too busy. We made up our history as we went along and it wasn't ever written down. It had stringent rules which did not need to be articulated.

I'd met Frank on a blind date after the war started: he was at Camp Atterbury near Columbus, Indiana. After a while, we knew we loved each other, but I wanted to be engaged and get married after the war. I think I was just scared because things were going too fast for me. But Frank said we'd either get married before he went overseas or we'd never see each other again. And I knew he wasn't going to change his mind. Anyway, I didn't dare risk it, so I told him we would get married, and it was a pretty reluctant answer to a proposal.

War time was no time for dithering about or hesitation. These soldiers were under so much pressure that they had no time for romantic dalliances. These decisions were thrust on thousands of us, maybe millions. The men, I think, needed to have the security of knowing someone who loved them was waiting at home. And as for the doom and gloom people who talked about these "war marriages that would never last," they were wrong. Hardly anyone I know who sent a man overseas later got a divorce. We were too glad to have them come home and they were too glad to get here.

The wedding was a hurry-up affair as so, so many of them were. My mother and I took a diamond to Mr. Edward Petri, the well known and trusted jeweler, downtown in Indianapolis. He said the stone was unflawed. What kind of a setting did I want? Then my mother took off her platinum guard ring, one she had had made from a platinum stick pin of her father-in-law's, and she said, "Can you set the ring on this?"

Mr. Petri seemed charmed by the idea and he and Mother seemed to be quite moved. They weren't weeping but they looked as if they might. Not me! I was going to get my engagement ring!

Frank was in southern Missouri getting a Signal Company ready to go overseas, and I was home in Indianapolis. He couldn't possibly get leave. He had given me a budget and told me to buy the ring myself. This was no time for stardust and black velvet boxes and a full moon.

Frank and I talked on the phone that night and I told him all about the ring. Then I said, "Honey, I paid twenty dollars more than you told me to and I'm awfully sorry."

A roar from the other side of the library door: Daddy putting in his two cents. "If that 'little bird' gave you a specific amount, you're too extravagant. So is your mother."

Daddy's terms of endearment were "fish," "bird," "little bird," and "socks." And he always shamelessly eavesdropped, so I just didn't pay any attention.

And I eavesdropped too. When Frank asked Daddy for my hand, he said, "Sir, I have eleven hundred dollars in the bank and my future is very uncertain."

There was so much urgency then for us. There wasn't time to fall in love, get engaged, be married, plan for the future, and have fun for work and play. Our marriages did not yet have that emotional glue, those special things, a word, a phrase, a bar of music, or a catch word, gossamer threads but unbreakable. They last beyond the grave. Things were so hurried that we didn't have time for gentle nurturing.

The women of World War II are now old and one of the main disadvantages for us and our listeners is how much we forget. Some of us even forget what we're saying in the middle of saying it. Then, the other one laughs and reminds us of what we were talking about and we get back on track. But there is one thing we will never forget. Ask any woman of any age what her husband's serial number is and she'll reel it off instantly. I am as sure of this as I am of anything in the world.

I had promised my mother that I wouldn't get married after a double holiday. Once again, someone else decided when we would get married. Does anyone remember those huge posters with the picture of Uncle Sam, pointing his finger and saying, "I want you!"? He meant it. We were married on a Monday afternoon, January 3, 1944, at the Tarkingtons' house on North Meridian after Christmas and New Years holidays. Frank was the only man in uniform at his wedding. His officers couldn't get leaves, and his family couldn't make the hard trip, and my family's men were in the service. His best man was the eleventh choice.

When I arrived at the house, I went to the kitchen before going upstairs to get dressed for the wedding. Aunt Susanah Tarkington was standing behind a table on which there was a huge bowl of champagne punch. She had a bottle of brandy in each hand and was upending them into the punch bowl. "Gilmore says this is our usual recipe, but I think it needs some pepping up." I looked at Gilmore, the butler, who was standing behind her. He rolled his eyes back in his head and gave me a grin that split his face.

I was told that the wedding was lovely. The best man and Gilmore saw to it that lots of peppy punch was passed around.

We went back to my parents for supper, where I guess everyone but the newly-weds still felt peppy. There was lots of singing. Gilbert and Sullivan got a workout that evening. "Into the family you'll be led . . . to seek the felicity that marriage grants . . . and these are your sisters and your cousins and your aunts." And sung lugubriously, "Oh a soldier's lot is NOT a happy one."

We were leaving at eleven-thirty to go to Ithaca, New York, to see Frank's family, whom I'd never met. He and I took a cab to the Athletic Club to pick up his suitcase. I planned to wait for him in that room on the east side of the lower floor, but that was not to be. Here they came, sisters, cousins, aunts and more, and herded me into the Athletic Club bar, the Trophy Room. Two men who were in there already seemed very interested in the diversion our group provided when they sang the songs they'd already sung back at our house. While they were singing and no end taken with themselves, Frank beckoned to me from the door and we fled. He had a taxi waiting and we headed for the Union Station. He said fervently, "Thank God, we've finally lost them."

We had not lost them. Suddenly there were horns honking. There were three cars full of merry makers and one got in front, one at the side and one at the back. So we were trapped, but our cab let us off in front of the station and they had to find parking places. When we opened one of the big doors, we saw the huge station packed wall to wall with people. No gaiety here, families seeing their men off to war, spending every last moment they had together. Just a murmur of tired anxious voices. The depression was almost palpable. I think any one of the people there could have agreed exactly with the words that Frank spoke to my father when he asked for my hand. "My future is very uncertain."

Our friends and relatives were about to change the sombre atmosphere with a roar of joy. We were still in the doorway. They opened both the big doors and made a "V," like migrating geese. By then we were kind of huddled in the middle as they charged into the mob, Moses parting the Red Sea. One of the men tenderly picked a sleeping infant from a bench and laid it in the lap of a surprised lady who was not its mother. Then he stood on the arm rests and gave three piercing whistles with two fingers between his teeth. "We have a bride and groom here. Let's have three cheers," he shouted. He need not have shouted, as the crowd was temporarily stunned into silence by the whistles, but the cheers that followed nearly took off the high roof of the building.

I don't know whether there is a formula or an equation for spontaneous combustion, but I've seen it happen and I've heard it happen. Did eyes of strangers meet, or were there questioning, tentative grins on some faces? I don't know but everything exploded at once. Fatigue lifted, feet stopped hurting and hearts stopped hurting, too. There was some sort of alchemy or infusion that happened to everyone there at the same time. It translated itself instantly into real gaiety and fun, and gaiety and fun were in short supply in January of 1944. The Invasion was only months away and troop ships were slipping out from all the ports on the East Coast, forming into convoys guarded by destroyers and cruisers and heading for England. Before the Invasion there were about 1.7 million allied service men in England. No wonder their hosts complained about the "Yanks" who were "Over-paid, over-sexed and over here."

The man who had led the cheers yelled, "Let's sing. I'll take requests in order." "Mairzy Doats" yelled someone and then started the biggest, loudest sing-a-long in the history of the Western World. About three thousand voices. They were the songs we sang around the campfires of Leland as the sun sank over the North Manitou and hits from the radio too: "Chattanooga Choo Choo," "Deep in the Heart of Texas," "I'm Looking Over a Four Leaf Clover," "Don't Sit Under the Apple Tree," "Amapola," "Tangerine," "The Sunny Side of the Street," "Pack Up Your Troubles," "You Are My Sunshine," and of course, "If You Knew Susie," and "Oh Susanah." Enough songs to sing for three hours with no repetitions.

Frank and I were separated in the mob and I wriggled myself to the outer edges of it. There I saw a curious sight; about six service men shoulder to shoulder and in a semicircle facing outwards. I peeked over a shoulder and saw a very tired, very teary young woman nursing her baby. One of the young men said to me, "She couldn't get into the ladies room. It's probably closed for the duration. Damn the war."

Yes, damn the war. Still it was the only reality we had. Trains constantly rumbled overhead, never our train. But after each train departure the mob thinned out a bit. Well, it thinned out to be just a big crowd so there was enough room to dance. The dancing didn't necessarily follow the tempo of the songs. In fact, it never did. But who cared?

My sister, who had been in our wedding, didn't take an active part in the sing-a-long, but she stood on a bench and watched and she has a retentive memory. (She thought all wedding send-offs were like this and was very let down at the conventional ones she was a part of after our own riotous one.) She told me later that there was a conga line snaking its way around the edges of the crowd, led by one of the men who'd been in the Athletic Club bar and who had followed the fun to the Union Station. He was ingenious. When the line was halted by people, he yelled, "Reverse and 1, 2, 3, kick." He even could lead his line sideways. From her perch, Babe could see everything. And she told us about two dancers we never saw at all. A short, muscular sailor with his sailor hat jammed to his eyebrows jitterbugged with a portly lady with blue hair. Babe reported that she dropped her fur coat on the floor, kicked off her high heeled shoes and then yelled at her partner, "Tell me what I'm supposed to do." He'd shout, "Turn around three times and then I'll pull you back, then you do it to me. Atta girl, hon." Hon was a fast learner. She yelled, "Throw me between your legs but don't let go." He obliged. After their dance she was panting. Delighted she yelled, "Why can't Herb dance like that? Let's do it some more." They did. The second man from the Athletic Club did a strenuous Charleston with a young woman in the uniform of the WAVES.

Frank and I, both limp with exhaustion, eventually found each other and a bench to sit down on. We held hands and watched the tumult with glazed eyes. Thank heavens they'd forgotten us. There was no peppy punch down here at the station, but hundreds of happy drunks. They were drunk from having fun. FUN may be an understatement, but the war was temporarily forgotten and the sky was the limit.

There was a kind of joyous bedlam, and all the people seemed to have an inexhaustible supply of adrenaline or whatever it was. But Frank and I were running on "empty." It took me a long time to come full-circle about this bedlam—to be glad it happened instead of cringing as the decibels mounted and the chance that Frank and I would be alone diminished in direct ratio to the noisy happiness.

After several centuries our train was announced. The crowd remembered us and started on "Rock-A-Bye-Baby." Everyone who could get onto the stairs leading to the platform did so. And of course they also went up the "down staircase," not so much in a rush as a surge. An unstoppable rush of people and as many as could getting on the train. Our porter, may the gods smile on him, looked at us and said, "I'll get rid of 'em for you." He yelled "All aboard," about three times and they backed out reluctantly. Our Pullman was unheated and heading into the teeth of a blizzard. We didn't take our coats off it was so cold. Army overcoats are so bulky they need a berth of their own. In the morning the blanket was littered with Kleenexes and we'd both caught terrible colds. I so wanted to look my best when I met my new in-laws, and not like a person with a runny nose who had slept in her clothes.

Two days after we'd arrived in Ithaca the telegram that Frank was pretty sure was coming, came. "All leaves cancelled. Report to Camp Crowder within forty-eight hours."

Going back to Indianapolis we had the same porter we'd had leaving three nights ago and he filled us in on what happened at the station after we'd left. He told us about his friend Harry, a porter in the next car. He went off duty in Indianapolis. "Harry can't rest when there's singin' and always has his harmonica in his pocket. He played for 'em. He say, 'I played "On the Banks of the Wabash," because they might get homesick, then "Onward Christian Soldiers," and that he say, really did take the roof off. He had to play that one twice. Then he played 'Abide With Me,' and as the cleaning crew came in, 'Auld Lang Syne.' Harry he thinks deep. He say, 'Why do there have to be war to make folks friendly.' He told 'em about a place to get coffee around the corner and he say, 'That station old and frumpy but she kicked up her heels that night.' And just like my daddy say, 'Singin' together helps feelin' scared.' True, too. Those folks singin' seemed happy. A good thing to see. Those folks just needed to have some fun."

Last year as we approached our fiftieth anniversary, I found I had come full-circle about our sendoff. I thought about that night and the people. Did any of them remember it? Did the husband of the young girl with the baby come home to them? Did she ever have civilian protectors as understanding as the men who shielded her as she fed her baby? Was the gaiety of that night the last fun that many of those people had till the war was over? And did Hon get Herb to jitterbug? Did the people who left the station arm in arm for coffee stay in touch with each other? I hope so.

And I was really glad that Frank and I were the unwitting catalysts that helped all those people to have their sing-a-long.

Years later after the Union Station had been tarted up, my sister's husband, an attorney, was a host for the annual Seventh Federal Circuit Court Association meeting and Babe showed their wives the sights. The Union Station was the highlight of the sightseeing trip. The ladies exclaimed with delight over the shops, boutiques, bars, restaurants, tourist traps, and cutie pie souvenir booths.

One woman said to Babe, "I can't imagine what this old place was like before it had these shops. It's bigger than a football field. You'd have to shout as loud as you could to make a person at the other end of the station hear you. Were you ever here before—when it was an old wreck, I mean before it was fixed up?"

"Yes, and you didn't have to shout. Just sing." I can just see my sister's face and the puzzled look of the visiting wife as Babe said, "There was a vaulted ceiling about a half a mile high, maybe sort of like a cathedral ceiling and there are probably echoes of songs still up there."

Babe forgot the visiting ladies and her role as their guide. While they shopped for knick-knacks, she too, suddenly had focused kaleidoscopic vision. As she hummed the first line of, "Onward Christian Soldiers," she thought, "Oh, ladies, ladies, if you only knew what I know. In January of 1944 there were about three thousand people who had never met each other before singing and dancing and hugging. But you'd never believe me, not in a million years!"

Just after the wedding we reported to camp. Brides who became "camp followers" found it very character building. It was to be a short, harried introduction into "going to housekeeping." We lived in Joplin, Missouri, thirty-five miles from Camp Crowder where Frank was stationed. There was one hotel in town which we couldn't afford for more than three days. So I hired a taxi and got the list of vacancies from the morning paper. Except for a couple of addresses, all the places were already rented and the cab driver refused to drive me down two streets because it was the "red light" district. Finally, through the Chamber of Commerce, I found a little house which had been a "mom and pop" grocery store before it was abandoned. "Abandoned" is the operative word about this house. The furnishings were minimal. Frank could only get home four nights a week. The only bus for Camp Crowder, thirty-five miles away, left at five o'clock in the morning and was a long walk from our house, and Frank could not miss that bus! For several nights we nervously clutched each other, waking up and asking, "What time is it now?" Finally my mother found a beat-up old kitchen clock with an alarm for us. Among other shortages, there was one of alarm clocks.

Our refrigerator was gas, and lighting the pilot light was a real challenge. I didn't know whether gas fumes would ruin food or not. One evening we decided that the house seemed awfully damp. Frank opened the old fashioned cellar door in the back yard and the whole basement was full of water, up to the top step. He just shut the door and we went back inside. Since we didn't have a car, I had to walk to the grocery store, about a mile away. I didn't know what to buy because I really couldn't cook anything, and I didn't understand the ration stamps system, and the butcher hated me. Missouri then had another piece of money called a "mill." Ten mills were equal to a penny. They looked like gray nickels and were plastic. Somehow mills almost did me in. I spent a lot of time getting taxis to take me to movies. The isolation was a bit dreary. When I got a case of the flu, Frank tried to get me into the hospital at the Post but he couldn't, so I lay on the couch and listened to the gentle lapping of the water in the basement. I was homesick, not for my new husband, but for my mother and my own bed.

A couple of weeks before we left Joplin, a soldier and his wife came to Camp Crowder. Stan was in Frank's Company and they had a car! Twice a week his wife was able to use it and she and I went to the grocery and just learned how to like each other because we both had been lonely.

Since she had had me for dinner, I invited her to come to our house for supper. Both men were in camp that night. "I'll just go in and get things started," I said. But she followed me into the kitchen. I opened a can of salmon and dumped the contents into boiling water. Letha's eyes got bigger but she didn't laugh.

"I'll tell you what," she said finally. "Let's drain the water out of the fish and we can have salmon burgers. Where is your colander?"

"What's a colander?"

"Well, never mind. Just hand me the sieve."

"I don't have one."

We ended up with layers and layers of toweling with greasy, oily salmon on it. She mixed it with some flour, salt, and pepper. The mixture stuck together, and it was edible— barely.

The next day a ham arrived sent by my mother and I called Letha to ask her what to do with it. She said very firmly, "Don't do anything to it! But bring it over right this minute and we'll eat here tonight. The boys will be home." Her dinner was delicious with sweet potatoes, a ham sauce, salad, and some brownies which Mother had also sent us.

About thirty years ago Letha and her husband were coming through Indianapolis and came out to visit us— but not for dinner. By then I could finally laugh at myself, and so could Letha.

My mother, through a friend of a friend, had given me a Joplin lady's phone number. I called her up and her response was glacial. The day before we left Joplin she called me back. I expect it took all that time for her to check me out. She asked me to lunch and to knit. In our war, women were always knitting something for soldiers. I told her my husband was going overseas and I couldn't come.

"Oh, I feel so guilty that I haven't called you before."

"That's your problem." I tried to be as glacial as she was, but then I began to cry. I said, "You could at least have been polite or kind to me when I called you, and I wasn't going to steal your silver," and I hung up on her. If only she had called me up early on, my Joplin days would have been very different.

When she called, I was packing up our things while Frank was getting final orders at Camp Crowder. I had been packing as if I were doing it for someone else, not for me, and I was trying desperately not to think ahead. But her call taught me my lesson number one in World War II. Try hard not to be so skinless and vulnerable, and don't cry when you are angry. This lesson didn't take with me. It's more than fifty years later and I still haven't learned how to be angry without crying.

Half an hour later I was at the electric company settling up our bill.

I said to the girl behind the counter that my husband was going overseas and she burst into tears and said, "So's mine." And we cried and hugged each other. Scenes like this were common.

Frank and I stood in the rain waiting for my train to Indianapolis. He put me on the train, and he got on a troop train going to his POE (Port of Embarkation.) He had said to keep a suitcase packed in case he were at the POE for a week or so. If we were lucky we could meet in New York.

I came home and reluctantly joined the passion of my sisters of the World War II generation. There were so many of us.

I didn't hear anything from him for nine weeks. He had evaporated. As his train pulled into the POE, security was clamped down, no calls, no mail—and the convoy went out the next day. It was the biggest convoy of the war, about three-hundred ships, and they only saw one other ship—the Queen Mary. Her insides had been stripped out for the war and she could carry 3,000 men. She never was in a convoy, never zig-zagged, and she was too fast for the Nazi submarines.

I had not even seen a trace of Leland over the previous summer. Instead I'd gone to business school and then to work in a defense plant. Now I went back to work at Electronics Laboratories on west New York Street, the place where I had worked before I was married. I was secretary to the head of the order department, three men and four war wives. Needless to say, we outnumbered the gentlemen in more ways than one. I was secretary to a nice boss, Mr. J.R. Parlette. He used to glance at me over his glasses as I was busily typing and say, "After you have finished writing to Frank, do you suppose you could take a couple of letters?" Sometimes I could and sometimes I couldn't. When he began to trust me enough, he'd hand me a bunch of letters to be answered and say, "Tell them yes, tell them no, tell them soon, and pad it all out." He had been in the Army but serious eye trouble was discovered when he was on the rifle range and he was honorably discharged.

I had one serendipity while I worked there. My roommate in college worked for the Office of Strategic Services (OSS, later the CIA), in Washington, and I had to call them on business. I knew she worked there so I just asked for her extension and she answered the phone and we talked almost every day.

Once when she was home on a vacation, she and her mother had the same dream one night. Her brother, Donny, badly wounded, was rolling down a hill and his eyes were shut. Later, when he came home he told them that they had dreamed an actual event.

Electronics Laboratories didn't actually manufacture anything. The only secret thing I ever heard of was called the "black light" — a light that softly illuminated the control panels of planes that flew at night so that the pilot's night vision was not impaired. It was of course very top secret and their one contribution to the war effort.

One day my mother called me at work to say, "You have twenty-one letters from Frank." I cried with joy and looked at my very nice boss. "Okay," he smiled at me, "and you can use my car but don't speed or wreck it. And in payment, you have to read one letter aloud." But I didn't do that.

Before that I had had the same frustrating dream every night. I knew that I was married and Frank was away fighting in a war, but when I told people no one believed me. After that letters came fairly regularly and I stopped having the dream. My brother was in England flying in the B-17s that bombed Germany, and our dear postman, Elmer, pushed the doorbell twice for a letter from Frank and once for a letter from Johnny, so Mom could rush from any place in the house and pick up the mail. One day towards the end of the war, Elmer rang and came in to tell us that he had asked to work in the downtown post office building. He gave his reasons and we couldn't blame him. He said, "I just delivered five letters to the Fountains. They're from their boy who was killed last month."

One of the unspoken rules among war wives was that if you were getting letters from your husband or sweetheart and someone else wasn't, of course you never mentioned yours. About six weeks before June 6, 1944, no one got any mail. England was closed up tight. The Invasion of France was imminent.

Of course none of us really knew whether our husbands would go in on D-Day or not. The wives of infantry men were nearly paralyzed with fear. My God, it was so scary. The morning of June 6th, 1944, at five AM, my Leland friend Lutie Appel called and I knew before I answered the phone what she would say, "The invasion has begun."

As I stood on the crowded bus on D-Day morning, somebody started singing a song made famous by Kate Smith, "Praise the Lord and Pass the Ammunition," and we followed it with the "Battle Hymn of the Republic." Many were in tears. That noon all the church doors were wide open. Lutie and I went to Christ Church on the Monument Circle. There were no flowers, no organ, no priest, just kneeling women. When the pews filled up, people knelt on the floor and we grabbed the hand of someone we had never known before. Maybe we were circling our wagons against the terror. The bells in the steeple were playing hymns like "Onward Christian Soldiers," "The Battle Hymn of the Republic," and "Rock of Ages," hymns that are stirring whenever they are heard. That noon their message came into every heart. Prayers were almost palpable in the air.

Terror is a great leveler. I still remember thinking then, I guess it was for the first time, that a lot of women who were kneeling here, would not have their prayers answered. Every prayer I think must have been the same. "God, please keep him safe." Frank's mother was a firm Christian and her faith never faltered for one instant, so I sometimes held on to hers when mine was feeling weak.

From then on, our lives were filled with work and worry. The fear was always there, even in dreams. Casualty lists started being printed in the newspapers. There were occasionally things that absolutely undid us, and we could never anticipate them. It might be the sight of a Christmas tree, seeing a new baby, even the Thanksgiving turkey. There were sudden tears sometimes, and too, terrible collapses of energy. Being always afraid is very tiring. While we waited, something queer happened to time. It stretched on forever. Two months seemed like six months. A year later it seemed just the same. It never got any better, it just stretched out farther.

Soldiers were given basic training and military exercises before they went overseas so they were somewhat prepared, but no one prepared us. One of the things that we wives did was exchange conversation with perfect strangers—saleswomen, bus conductors, waitresses, people on the bus, someone standing at a bus stop reading a paper and you read over his shoulder, or standing in line at the Post Office. We recognized each other instantly—some sort of stigmata that was invisible to the eye, but not to the heart.

We never, under any circumstances violated one another's privacy. Some of the war wives used to eat lunch together and one of the women had a husband in submarines. If you had a husband in that service, the submarine might just never come back. Later a telegram, "Missing—presumed lost." These messages were delivered by a boy in a Western Union uniform on a bicycle. To see one of them, even ten miles from your house was heart-stopping.

We knew what our friend must be feeling, but of course we never mentioned it and neither did she. I think she didn't dare mention it. She could become completely unraveled, and we prayed that didn't happen to any of us. Once someone stopped by the table and said to her, "What do you hear from Jim?" She smiled back at him and said, "Nothing right now, but I'm expecting something any day." At that time we had to make our marriages work simply by faith. Sometimes we couldn't even remember the sound of our husbands' voices. Their handwriting, though, was beloved, and we lived in the future. Every time I was particularly scared, I went and bought a small piece of furniture for our life after the war.

In December of 1944, the Dramatic Club of Indianapolis gave its Christmas dance. Some of the older members insisted that we war wives attend, something we certainly did not want to do, but we were manipulated into going. I think there were six or seven of us sitting at a little table feeling very dispirited and sorry for ourselves when we saw a couple dancing. Tom Werbe, in his Navy whites, was home on leave and dancing with his wife Barbara. They were both so tall and beautiful and they seemed to have a light all the way around them. Strangely enough, we didn't feel any searing envy at all that he had gotten a leave. We just all thought, "That can happen to me, too." I have never seen two such gloriously happy faces.

Betty McCafferty, about six months pregnant, worked in the Drafting department. Her husband was a paratrooper. He landed in France the night before the Invasion, and her telegram which came a month later said that he was missing in action and presumed dead. This brought the reality of war too close to home. Betty didn't faint or cry. She turned as white as chalk, put the telegram in her pocket and went on working. I walked over to the head of her department and hissed at him, "Don't touch her and don't talk to her right now, maybe later. Tell her to punch out and go home early if she wants too, and that's all." As we prayed for Betty's husband to be safe, and as the saying goes, "We pulled up our socks and got on with it." Got on with what? Got on with winning the war.

As news of the war increased, we lived by the radio when we were not working. This was not a war that anyone saw on television. Every night we listened to Edward R. Murrow starting off each time with "This is London," and Gabriel Heatter who said almost every night in his high pitched tone, "There's bad news tonight," and there usually was. During the war there was a cartoon in *The New Yorker* by George Price. A husband is looking angrily at the dented fender that his wife's carelessness has caused. She says, "I really didn't mean to, but I was turning the corner and on the radio Gabriel Heatter was starting to say something ominous."

We had someone very special who brought the war into our living room, a man who was born in Dana, Indiana, THE HOOSIER VAGABOND, Ernie Pyle! He covered the war the way the infantry soldier fought it: on the ground, on the move, subject to filth and fear, and fate that dealt death to one man and not to another. Ernie was with the infantry in North Africa, Sicily, Italy, France, and the Pacific and he lived with the men he wrote about. "All the war of the world has seemed to be borne by the few thousand front line soldiers here. Destined merely by chance to suffer and die for the rest of us." Pyle knew too, that "it was neither God, nor the Flag, nor Mother that compelled a pimply faced kid to risk his life in an obscene adventure. He did it for the kid next to him; he couldn't let him down. They needed each other so bad . . . I lay there in the darkness thinking of the millions faraway at home, who must remain forever unaware of the powerful fraternalism in the ghastly brotherhood of war."

He was with the First Infantry in North Africa and he wrote in a dispatch from Tunisia:

I wish you all could see one of the ineradicable pictures I have in my mind today . . . a narrow path comes like a ribbon over a hill miles away . . . all along the length of this ribbon there is now a thin line of men. For four days and nights they have fought hard, eaten little, washed none, and hardly slept at all. Their nights have been violent with attack, fright, butchery, and their days sleepless and miserable with the crash of artillery. The men are walking . . their walk is slow, for they are dead weary, as you can tell even when looking at them from behind. Every line and sag of their bodies speaks their inhuman exhaustion . . . . They don't slouch. It is the terrible deliberation of each step that spells out their appalling tiredness. Their faces are black and unshaven. They are young men, but the grime and whiskers and exhaustion make them look old.

In their eyes as they pass, is not hatred, not excitement, not despair, not the tonic of their victory - there is just the simple expression of being here as though they had been here doing this forever, and nothing else . . . the line moves on, but it never ends. All afternoon men keep coming round the hill and vanishing eventually over the horizon. It is one long tired line of ant-like men . . . there is an agony in your heart and you almost feel ashamed to look at them. They are just guys from Broadway and Main Street, but you wouldn't remember them. They are too far away now. They are too tired. Their world can never be known to you, but if you could see them just once, just for an instant, you would know that no matter how hard people work back home they are not keeping pace with these infantrymen in Tunisia.

Noble Dean, a dear Indianapolis friend of ours, flew Spitfires in the RAF over Africa. There were twenty-two planes in his group and only two men survived. He said that British understatement was true, at least in the skies over Africa. A flyer in his group took a hit—then said calmly over the radio, "It looks like I'm for it, Tally-ho chums." And his plane spiraled down to crash.

Noble's daughter, after his death, found his medals pushed to the back of one of his desk drawers. He had never told his children about them. What he did tell them was, that he was kept very busy ferrying whiskey for some VIPs. Of course there had been more to it than that.

Bill Cory, another Indianapolis friend, was taken prisoner in Northern Africa by General Rommel's forces. At first Bill said things in the POW camp were not too bad, but the prisoners were moved northward four different times and each camp was worse than the one before. From these moves they could guess how the war was going for the Germans. The Germans often had a man infiltrate the prisoners who were officers, to catch any hint of plans for escape. One day Bill was the officer in charge of looking for infiltrators, and a friend of his came and told him that they had found one. "All he'll do is give his name, rank and serial number." Bill went to see the prisoner and to everyone's surprise, they roared with laughter and hugged each other. It was his college roommate. Bill and several men escaped into the Baltic Corridor in January. All the peasants could give them to eat were rotten potatoes which they were eating themselves. Nothing smells much worse than a rotten potato, so the men must have been ravenously hungry. He caught a serious ear infection which of course was untreated and has given him lasting problems. For many months he couldn't eat a potato.

For some reason, I was sort of relieved that Frank had been sent into England, France and Germany, rather than to the Pacific. The first ghastly news we got was that of the Japs taking Corregidor. General MacArthur and General Wainwright, along with officers, men and nurses had fled to that huge rock in Manila Bay off the Philippines and they were fighting literally with their backs to the wall. A submarine came silently at night to take General MacArthur, his wife, his baby and his baby's nurse off the rock.

Now I knew in my heart that it was really right for MacArthur to go, he had too. But couldn't they have found room in that submarine for some of the Army nurses? Some of them were raped and beaten to death before they ever got off the rock, and others killed themselves. After that horrible carnage, the surviving men were marched to Bataan, in what is called the Bataan Death March, and it truly was. Many, many people did not survive because they were beaten to death on their way to the prison camp. General Wainwright looked old and feeble before he even went on the Bataan Death March. He did survive though, and once, several months after VJ Day, my mother was with a friend in Tiffany's in New York when General Wainwright came in with his wife to buy her pearls. The other customers huddled awestruck in the corner while they picked out the pearls. Then he walked over to my mother and her friend and a couple of other people and said, "Do you think these will do?" They couldn't speak for crying, but they clapped and smiled, as did his wife of course. He only lived for several months after this. His health had been completely broken. I did know the wife of another soldier who survived the Death March and the three years in a POW camp. However, as soon as he came back to the United States he had to enter a mental hospital, where he died.

In June of 1994, we celebrated the 50th Anniversary of D-Day and later Bill Moyers, the American journalist, traveled with some, well, old men in the bus, men who had been there in December 1944, back to Luxembourg where the Battle of the Bulge had started on December 16, 1944. He was talking to one of them who had won our country's highest honor, the Congressional Medal of Honor, and the man looked terribly surprised and said, "What's this about a goddamn medal? For God's sake, it was Georgie, my buddy out there wounded, and we'd been together since Omaha Beach. He coulda froze to death." His buddy was wounded in a mine field that was also being shelled and the temperature was somewhat below zero. Pyle also wrote,

You can scarcely credit the fact that human beings, the same people you've known all of your life, could adjust themselves so readily to a type of living that is only slightly above the cave man stage . . . I believe that in wartime your physical discomfort becomes a more dominant thing in your life than the danger you're in. The danger comes in spurts. The discomfort is perpetual. You're always cold and almost always dirty. Outside of food and cigarettes, you had absolutely none of the little things that made life normal back home . . . You used to be sore when you couldn't get a taxi. Now you have struck gold when you can find a spot where you can lie down out of the wind.

I know a man, now old like me who, when he was a brand new ensign in the Navy, treated himself to an expensive restaurant. He was seated at a table next to a private who was eating alone. He had frightful table manners, or maybe none at all, and shoveled peas into his mouth with a spoon and picked his teeth. My Leland buddy Jack Gilligan, from Cincinnati, felt very superior to this ill-mannered hillbilly. That is, he did, until the private got up to leave. Among his ribbons Jack saw a blue one with white stars. The Medal of Honor.

I lived with my parents and my younger sister during the time that Frank was overseas. I don't think I was a particularly cherished house guest either, but we all tried. Daddy began by informing me that since I was a married woman and had a job, I had to pay room and board. I was perfectly incensed at him and told him so. He kept on smiling and said, "Your board and room will be seven dollars a week, and you buy your own liquor." Just to annoy him I used to leave change on the big table in the living room and then I would say, "Daddy, there's one dollar and thirty-seven cents on this week's board." He would then curse and say, "That's no way to pay a debt." Then I would say, "If you don't want it, don't take it." One time I put fifty Missouri mills from Joplin, which were worth one nickel.

We also had some fun with each other, grabbing at anything that might be mildly entertaining. We each had our bottle of whiskey and eyed each other's bottle almost with magnifying glasses. We both marked how much we had drunk from our bottles. I didn't ever put water in his bottle, but I'm not so sure he didn't put it in mine.

During the two winters I was home, we couldn't get firewood, so we had a coal grate, and my mother put huge heavy curtains over the three French doors to keep the heat in. The fuel shortage was acute. The thermostat was set at 62 degrees, unless I'd come by and when no one was looking, would set it up to 75 for a few minutes.

We complained about how cold it was and then Daddy would say, "Not one person has gotten a cold all winter."

We did cherish occasional funny things. After my cousin Patty's husband had left for the ETO (European Theater of Operations), she came back to Indianapolis by train. She had reserved a drawing room and in it were she, her six month old baby, the baby's nurse, and a king-size French poodle. After the train started, the conductor opened the door to get her ticket. "Oh, dear, well, let me pay you now. I forgot to get it." Her money and the nurse's money didn't come to enough for a ticket and I don't think the conductor could exactly see pushing them off into the night, so he told her to pay at the Indianapolis ticket station. The poodle somehow rushed out while the door was opened and ended up two cars down in the club car where he certainly made a hit. He leaped over soldiers, chairs, and got on the bar and laughed in dog language, "Isn't this fun?"

When the train came into Indianapolis, Patty's father was waiting for them. Patty hugged him and said, "Pappy, I have to borrow a lot of money because I forgot to get my ticket and I didn't have enough money to buy one." He gave her some and she went to the ticket agent and paid her fare. Her father looked on with awe. "Patty, you are the only person I ever knew who had a charge account with the Pennsylvania Railroad."

Daddy and I packed care packages to be sent to Johnny and Frank. We picked up the cardboard boxes at the post office and put them together ourselves and then added the things that we wanted to send. Standing in line at the post office with one's care package was a wonderful way to make friends and get ideas for the care packages. We told each other what was in our boxes, where the men were, and anything else we could think of. If it were one ounce over five pounds the post office refused to take it and the postmaster said to me once, "They'll see that it's overweight and they won't send it back, they'll just ditch it or else eat what's inside." Care packages presented lots of challenges. I knew Frank was very fond of Canadian Club whiskey, but what to put it in? I finally, after lots of experiments, decided that a Milk of Magnesia bottle had the thickest glass and boiled out the magnesia part. Canadian Club came from president Garstang's secretary who bought him cigarettes and whiskey on the black market. We had to send things that weren't perishable because these packages went by a very slow boat. Crackers, cookies, cheese, candy, and cigarettes were good items.

Here at home, cigarettes were harder to find than gold. Once a week, at Electronics Laboratories, we were all given two packages of cigarettes which we guarded zealously. There were three smokers and four non-smokers in our office and the non-smokers were bribed and bribed. One day a good friend, Jack Rogers, walked into our office and gave me a full carton of Lucky Strikes. This was like finding the mother lode. During the war Lucky Strikes were a very popular brand of cigarettes. Mr. Parlette, my boss, offered me $100.00 for the carton, and cigarettes were selling for twenty-five cents a pack. No sale. I certainly could have used the one hundred dollars but this was for Frank. Of course later, I found out that in some areas they "liberated" lots of wine and were issued cigarettes. I sent Frank the best care present in the world which I found in Block's Boy Scout department, a Sterno stove called "canned heat." It was a little round metal container and the top of it was the size of a soup can or a cup. After I told people about it, there was a run on the Boy Scout department. After the War, Frank said, "You sent me so many kinds of cheese and spread, but never any crackers." Anyway, the dehydrated soup and water went wonderfully with it.

Once while I was at home, Daddy and I were fixing a Christmas care package. This was in August. We had found little trees and raided our family's Christmas ornaments for nonbreakable ones, and they looked pretty perky. As Daddy and I worked upstairs on my bed, my mother was downstairs cooking the kind of Christmas cookies that we have every year, and Bing Crosby was on two different radios singing "I'm Dreaming of a White Christmas." I don't think Daddy cried but I got a little teary and I went downstairs to get the cookies and found my mother dissolved in tears. She said, "Yes, but what Christmas will they be home for?"

My little sister says she remembers me pulling off my secretary's clothes and getting into a bubble bath with my letters and having a drink on the side of the bathtub. I'm sure she's right; I can't quite remember, but it certainly sounds like the nicest part of the day. And she and I took a walk after supper with Willkie, our springer spaniel.

After the walk with Willkie, the four of us had cutthroat games of quadruple solitaire. Keeping a routine seemed important, but we never mentioned it, and we never touched each other much. There was much love among us, but hugging, at least in my case, might bring tears and I couldn't risk it. Crying was dangerous for me. Things inside me that were barely glued together, got unglued completely. My father's biggest problem, after my board and room was, "Where in the hell is MY *Saturday Evening Post*?" I always grabbed it early and read it. There always was a serial which ran for about eight weeks and Daddy liked to read them all at once after the last issue. Invariably, at least one *Post* was missing. And he said it was always my fault. Well, it was!

Daddy and I enjoy a quiet moment on our stairs before the big event.

There were only three short days for our trip to French Lick. It was like that for so many of us.

Capt. Frank Mayberry somewhere in E.T.O. (1944)

Frank and I share a fleeting moment before he goes overseas.

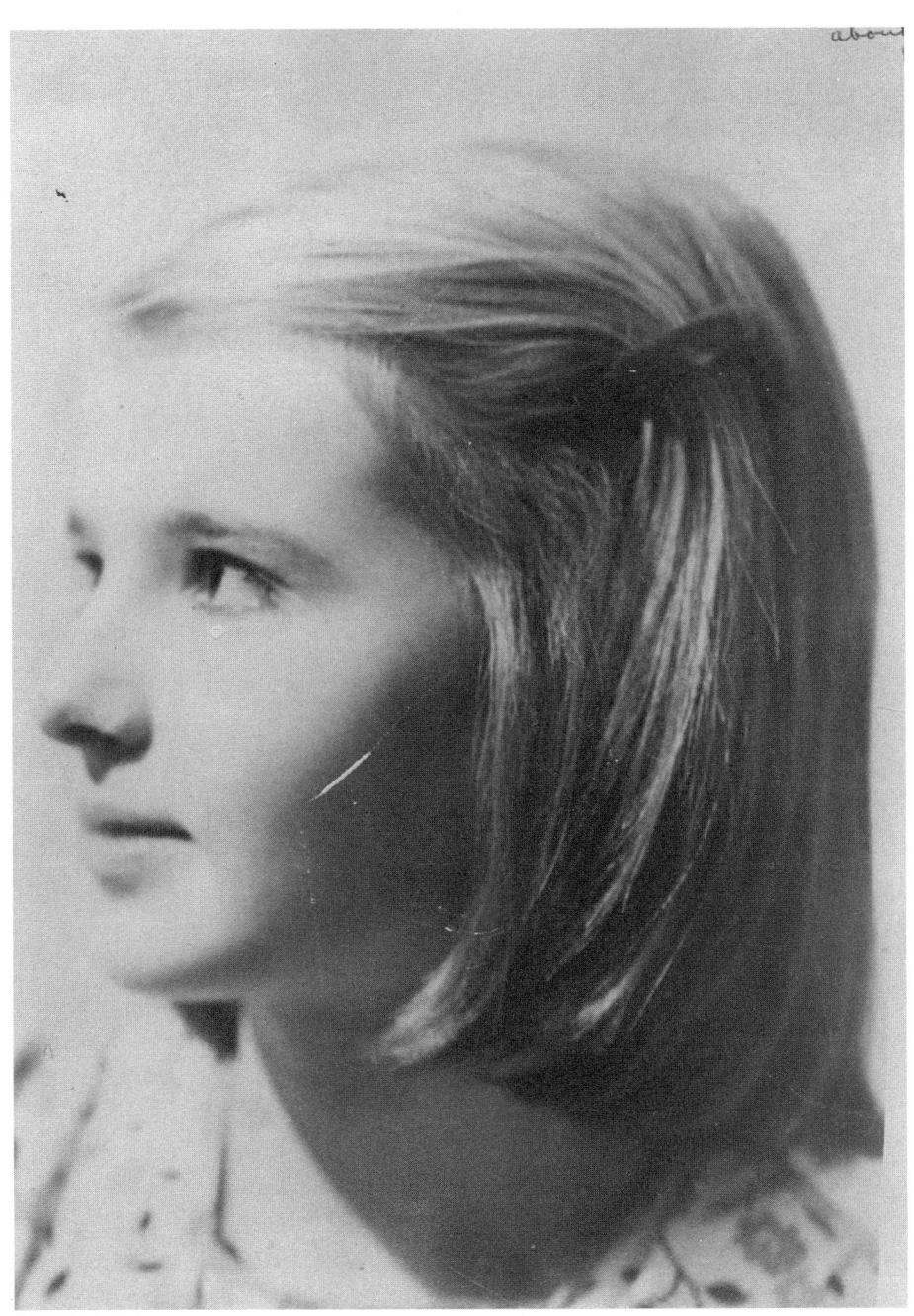

Sister Babe, my playmate, friend, and companion of Leland days and life beyond.

Daddy used to pick me up after work, which was a very, very kind thing for him to do because he usually went home at four o'clock for a nap before supper. I didn't get out until five-thirty. Early in April I told him that I had made out my taxes and I was taking Frank as a dependent. "Ye Gods, you'll end up in jail . . . you're bound to . . . it's absolutely illegal." "I hope not. I've also filed my return." Daddy thought I was a lunatic. He got together with his own CPA who looked through a lot of tomes trying to find out how much I was breaking the law, then the CPA said to my father, "I can't find anything in any of these books that it is really illegal, but John, it is damn unusual."

My father was devoted to his sister-in-law, a widow with two daughters. The older sister had two little children and her husband did work for a war plant that had regeared for war production. So Gene didn't have to join up, but Daddy took a chance when he talked sternly to Aunt Christine. "Gene ought to go to war. It's the great adventure of our time. And he'll always be sorry if he doesn't go."

Aunt Christine was distressed and angry, but my father went right on. "I eat lunch with the same men everyday, and if someone mentions World War I, the same few men drift away from the table, the ones who were not in it."

Gene did not go to war. He borrowed money from a very rich friend and started a small plant. He was hugely successful, but I have heard veterans say, "He got a five year head start." And I don't know whether he was sorry or not. I am sure he would have told me why he didn't go to war several years ago. But he was dying so I didn't ask him.

One summer when I was home my father insisted that we have a "victory garden." Victory gardens were the thing to do. You grew your own vegetables. Daddy took great pride in having ours in a square and he had cabbages planted on each side. Please bear in mind that my father had never touched a piece of cabbage or any slaw either. He never ate radishes because they gave him heartburn, and he didn't like beans. But, he wanted to eat some homegrown corn; so did the corn bores who had invaded the stalks of corn and the only thing we really got was tomatoes which we thought we should can. Then we were afraid of getting poisoned, so they rotted on the ground.

One day at work, the president, Mr. Garstang, and his brother-in-law Mr. Keevers, and his secretary, rushed into our office roaring as they came, "Where is it? What's happened to it?" And one of the secretaries said, "Maybe there is a spy, even." I said, in what I thought was my silkiest tone, "Are you talking about the invoices for the 'black light'?" One of them whirled at me and said, "How did you know it was called that?" And I said, "Well, it says so on the top page, and it's been on my desk for a couple of days, so I just filed it under "B." He grabbed it out, dropping half of the files on the floor, and rushed out. One of the men in the office looked at me and whispered loudly to the rest of them, "Do you think Mata Hara is in this office?" Then we exploded, and we laughed so hard people in Purchasing in the next office heard us and found out why, and they laughed too. It was just the kind of laughter which we had needed ever since Pearl Harbor, the kind that makes your stomach ache, and it did us all a world of good. My boss, when he could control himself said, "Wouldn't it make a wonderful comic strip?" It certainly would.

Mr. Keevers did not like the heat in our plant and neither did we. It was a one story, flat building with a tar roof, and of course there was no air conditioning. He had a lush, air conditioned office in the Circle Tower. One day I was sent over there to do some work, namely to balance his wife's checkbook. Allie Keevers, his wife, was a very stylish and expensively dressed woman, and I had met her several times before. She came in and said, "Susie, what on earth are you doing here?"

I smiled and said, "I work here. Right now I'm balancing your checkbook for you. Your husband asked me to. Do you want me to show you how to do it? Can you add and subtract?" She just said, "Oh. Well, no." She could not have done me more harm if she had done something to me on purpose. My status as a wartime secretary was badly bruised. Now everyone was going to know that I knew the wife of one of the bosses.

But one of the secretaries who liked me the least when I started to work there, began to notice me a little. She moonlighted as a teacher at Arthur Murray's Dance Studio. When she came dressed for "work," she was something. Her face wasn't so pretty, but she had the most gorgeous long legs and beautiful figure I have ever seen. She mentioned casually to me once, that usually someone from the dance studio came home with her. One day after we had gotten straight on the fact that I refused to do her filing for her, and I didn't appreciate her giving me the broken typewriter, she looked me up and down and then asked me if I would come to a party at her apartment the next Saturday. She said to come around midnight and that she lived at 16th and Illinois Street. Then she slowly looked me up and down again and said, "Well, no, I don't think you'd do." I didn't think I'd do either. Mr. Parlette heard this conversation and called me Elsie Dinsmore every chance he got when she wasn't in the room. He thought the whole thing was hilariously funny and that I would have been a very bad guest to have. "You'd probably get into a fight with one of the men because he didn't vote the Republican ticket. Or was an indispensable person." I said, "I can't imagine how Arthur Murray's studio can get any men at all for the studio." He raised his eyebrows at me and laughed and said, "I can." Then he added, "But I don't think they'd really be your type."

೧   ೧   ೧

The summer of 1944 I didn't go to Leland either. I was working full time, and somehow I didn't have a taste for that unchanging northwoods beauty. Still, the war ground on.

December 16, 1944, known now as the Battle of the Bulge. The fight was the biggest single battle in the history of World War II. I knew Frank was there. He had written, lying in his teeth, "There are nurses nearer the front than I am." The Germans, counting on bad weather, surprise, and a huge army, had struck the allied front with half a million men, the famous Fifth Panzer Division and even some untrained young boys. Frank told me about these youngsters and I asked him much later how he had seen them. He gave me an odd look and said,

"I only saw them after they were dead." This, as we were deluding ourselves that the Germans were almost beaten. During this period my Christmas box came home. The needles had fallen off the little tree and it seemed to me to be a terrible omen. I knew that Frank's outfit was practically next door to Bastogne, and later he told me after he had gotten home, that they had lost radio contact with Patton's Third Army and eventually got a message that said in effect, "Retreat or stay put—your choice." Frank, the CO, decided that his company would stay put. Other war wives were getting letters during the Battle of the Bulge which lasted into January, but of course they pretended that they weren't. I was so afraid that I could hardly stand it, and what do you do if you can't stand it. You just do. That's all. My own family was wonderful to me, and we didn't discuss what Frank was doing at all, but we certainly listened to every radio commentator, and no one hugged me. Mr. Parlette didn't play by the rules. He hugged me as I came in one day and said, "I'm sure Frank's all right." Tears. One night during the Battle of the Bulge we went over to the Tarkingtons for an evening visit. Uncle Booth, ruefully laughing, said, "Frank Mayberry has to be the busiest man in Europe right now. Moving all that equipment to the rear. I can hardly imagine any harder duty. I hope his NCO's are good men." I guess I smiled. Anyway, I didn't burst into tears. Those days were infinitely long. When you have such fear, when you wake up before you're entirely awake, you feel something pressing down on you. Something's wrong but what is it? After I was really awake, I felt sick with terror.

We always had Christmas dinner at our house. This year, two people wouldn't be there. While we were having dinner, a cousin of mine said to me, "Has Frank gone overseas yet?"

Granted, it was a stupid remark, and she probably didn't even know there was a war, but my fuse was very, very short. Maybe she didn't mean any harm, at least now I think maybe she didn't. I started to get up. (It was her husband that Daddy thought should go to war.) All of my leg muscles were ready for me to leap across the table and strangle her. I didn't think "I'll kill her," I was on my way to do it! I was sitting next to my father at the table and he knew something was very wrong. He grabbed my arm so tightly I had bruises from his grip. Then he told a dumb joke to get everybody off the subject of the war and nodded his head imperceptibly and I took this to mean that I could excuse myself.

I walked over to Lutie Appel's house and we took a two-hour walk in the snow. Lutie laughed and said, "This has been a great day for everybody. I've just been talking to Ellie who is in hysterics."

"Bad news?" I asked.

"Oh no, her step-mother just told her she couldn't hang her stockings and underwear over the shower pole in the guest bathroom." And no one even used it. Was there ever such a place as the Appel cottage? The Jameson place near quiet waters? Leland seemed very far away indeed.

Finally the weather broke and the bombers could fly out of England. Frank later said that they heard the noise before they saw the planes. Ernie Pyle described it. "The sound was like a surge of doom. It was the heavys! At first they were dots in the sky and they came with a terrible slowness in flocks of twelve. Three flights to a group and in groups that stretched across the sky." Frank abandoned caution, stood up in his foxhole and yelled, "Give 'em hell, Johnny!"

Our family doctor had enlisted early in the war and he parachuted into Bastogne in Belgium. He went in with the 101st Airborne. This town was ringed by German troops and it was from here that General McAuliffe allegedly said to the German general who demanded their surrender, "Nuts!" I asked our doctor if he was awfully scared to parachute and he said a two syllable word which needed no explanation. After he started taking care of the wounded he forgot to be afraid. While he was fixing splints for two compound fractures, the boy next to him quietly bled to death. He told me that he sometimes had nightmares and he could see the dead boy's face looking at him.

The Germans had bombed the cathedral in Coventry, England, a very beautiful and famous cathedral. There were no military objectives anywhere around it. Before they bombed it, the English had cracked the German code and learned that they were planning to bomb Coventry. They did not protect the Cathedral or the buildings, or warn the civilians. Had they done so, the Germans would have known that they had cracked the code. A lot of innocent civilians died to keep that secret.

When they could, after the war, the British built another Coventry Cathedral out of the wreckage that was left by the bombs. The Allied fire bombing of Dresden has been thought of as a dastardly trick. Sure it was, but so was Coventry.

One bitterly cold Sunday in January, with the Bulge Battle still raging, I took a bus to the Murat Theatre to hear Arthur Rubenstein play. I thought maybe I could lose some of my fears listening to his music. The first half was just fine. In the second part the pianist played a Chopin nocturne. He may have played more than one, but I wasn't there. Those pure notes somehow undid me. I had, for my own sake and the sake of others, tried to appear calm and brave, but the tears streamed. I stumbled to the lobby and stood crying with my forehead leaning against the wall, and I couldn't stop until a timid hand touched my shoulder and a voice said, "It didn't work, did it?" I shook my head because I couldn't talk yet. "Is it Belgium?" I nodded.

"Me, too. Let's go somewhere and get a cup of coffee." The girl and I talked for a long time and exchanged first names, but that's all. We didn't need to say any more. We already knew each other to the bone.

After the war Frank's boss and his wife were spending an evening with us and Ned remembered that during the Battle of the Bulge period, from his foxhole he saw a group of MPs marching German prisoners. There was a POW headquarters that was down the road. As they rounded the curve, Ned could no longer see them but he heard a volley of shots and MPs came back up the road whistling "Jingle Bells."

No one had forgotten that the Germans killed I don't know how many wounded and unarmed soldiers in a nearby forest, Malmedy, near where Frank was stationed. When his letters started coming again, they were cryptic, but no matter. He was alive.

Ernie Pyle spoke of a conversation he had had with a noncom, he was called the "Old Man," and his age was twenty-four years. He spoke of infantry replacements. "I know it ain't my fault that they get killed, and I do the best I can for them . . . but I just hate to look at them when the new ones come in. Some of them have just got fuzz on their faces and they're scared to death."

In our family we had a young cousin, Roy Miller, who was my brother's age. He was an infantry replacement and he was killed almost immediately.

Meanwhile, back at Electronics Laboratories, one sunny morning in April, Helen, who operated the switchboard, did whatever operators have to do so their words can be heard in absolutely every office and said, "Now hear this. Betty McCafferty's husband is fine and he is on his way home."

Forty-odd war wives stopped typing, filing, taking dictation, or whatever they were doing and we left. No one suggested it. We just did it. I had been taking dictation. I smiled at my boss and said, "Bye, I don't know when I'll be back." He smiled back and said, "Don't hurry." All of us filed past Ivory Adair, the beautiful black guard whom we loved so much and he opened the door for us, grinning from ear to ear. We headed towards the nearest bar, and it was only about eleven o'clock in the morning. After we got seated, Betty began to cry. She said, "This is the first time that I really have broken up, but just think, Harry is going to see his son now, and I was afraid he never would."

A few weeks later Betty brought her two Harrys to show us. Her husband was a tall, gangly redhead who obviously adored his wife. He was very shy and embarrassed. Betty was radiant and most of us touched her for luck. As I recall, Harry only spoke once and it was something like, "Y'all shouldn't make such a fuss over me."

Oh, yes we should!

The morning after our abdication Mr. Paulette said to me, "You had a long distance phone call while you were out. I had to get the phone because there wasn't anybody in the whole damn plant to answer it. A voice said, 'Susie, you just have to hear this,' and started right in talking. Later on, I said to her, 'You are mistaken, Miss. I'm Susie's boss and she is out drinking.'"

He went on, "She said that she wanted to come and work for me and asked how many liquor breaks there were in a day. She said that at the OSS (Office of Strategic Services) they run a very tight ship and she thinks it would be nicer here. She is a very fresh young lady and she sounds cute. She gave me a new extension number and wants you to call her today. Talk about scams, you two have a big one going. By the way, how often do you talk to her?"

"Only three or four times a week."

"She really couldn't stop thinking about all the drinking you were doing and, made a correct comment which was, 'I can see who runs that plant.' I told her she was right and you'd call her back some time today."

VE DAY—MAY 8, 1945

At our house we certainly did celebrate VE Day (Victory in Europe). At least it meant that my brother Johnny would not be flying any more missions. I wasn't so sure about Frank's immediate future because the war with Japan had not been won yet and Frank was afraid that he might be sent to invade the mainland. He and his company were in France then for R&R. I was so used to being afraid, I thought he'd fall into a manhole in Paris.

Frank wrote me on VE Day, "Darling, this is the day everyone in Europe has waited for so long . . . Cannes celebrated with cannon fire, sirens, bells, and dancing in the street. For them the war is really over.

For us, it might be just beginning. God help us. The civilians are jubilant and the soldiers are pleased, but of course we dread to hear about our possible new assignment."

Could we wives wait and worry for many more years? It looked as if we would have no choice, so of course we could.

When Pyle wrote this dispatch from the Pacific he said . . .

My heart is still in Europe and that's why I'm writing this column on VE Day. It is to the boys who were my friends for so long, and wondering why it is that I was not with them when it ended. The companionship of two and a half years of death and misery is a spouse that tolerates no divorce. Such companionship finally becomes a part of one's soul and it cannot be obliterated. Those soldiers who are still living have had burned into their brains the unnatural sight of cold dead men scattered over the hillsides and in the ditches along the high rows of hedge along the road throughout the world. These are the things that you at home need not even try to understand. To you at home they're columns and figures, for he is a dear one that went away and just didn't come back. You didn't see him lying so grotesque and pasty beside the gravel road in France. We saw him, saw him by the multiple thousands. That's the difference . . . .

Long after the war I became a good friend of Chester Minton, one of the priests at St. Paul's Episcopal Church in Indianapolis. Father Minton had been a chaplain in the South Pacific, and he told me that he had buried Ernie Pyle. Ernie Pyle was on a small island called Ie

Shima. He went out into a fox hole having been advised that the island was not completely secured, and there were undoubtedly Jap snipers. Ernie Pyle stood straight up in the foxhole and he was killed immediately. According to Chester, he deliberately did this so he would be shot, and Chester based this on the fact that Ernie Pyle had been through Africa, France, Germany, and Italy without getting a scratch. Our generation still mourns for Ernie Pyle.

I personally think, and I think other people would agree with me, that Pyle's writings helped to refuel and encourage the unity of the American people. From him we learned things we never could have imagined. Pyle was never on a balcony looking down, he was in a fox hole looking up, and he was scrupulous about including the names and addresses of servicemen that he had talked to. Also, I think he wanted to make it very plain to us at home that the boy who left home thinking that murder and killing was a sin was turned into one who knew that killing was a craft to those who practiced it.

Ensign William Evans, from Indianapolis, flew a torpedo plane off the *USS Hornet*, an aircraft carrier. He was killed at the Battle of Midway, as was his entire group, Group 8. Three Japanese carriers were sunk within eight minutes. Before the battle he wrote to an older friend in New England . . . .

The fates have been kind to me. In a war where any semblance of pleasure is to say the least, bad taste, I find many that would please you. When you hear others saying harsh things about American youth, know how wrong they all are. So many times now that it has become commonplace I've seen incidents that make me know that we were not soft or bitter; perhaps stupid at first but never weak. The boys who brought nothing but contempt and indifference in college—who showed an apparent lack of responsibility—carry the load now with a pride no Spartan ever bettered.

Many of my friends are now dead. To a man, each died with a nonchalance that each would have denied was courage. They simply called it lack of fear, and forgot the triumph. If anything great or good is born of this war, it should not be valued in the colonies we may win nor in the pages historians will attempt to write, but rather in the youth of our country who never trained for war, rather almost never believed in war, but who have from some hidden source, brought forth a gallantry which is homespun it

is so real.
I say these things because I know you liked and understood boys, because I wanted you to know that they have not let you down. That out here, between a spaceless sea and sky, American youth has found itself and given itself so that at home, the spark may catch, burn into flame and burn high. If the country takes these sacrifices with indifference, it will be the cruelest ingratitude the world has ever known . . .

My luck can't last much longer, but the flame goes on and on—that is important. Please give all my best wishes to all of the family, and may all you do find favor in God's grace.

Bill.

The war has such long, long memories for those who participated. About fifteen years ago a man was repairing a crack in our library ceiling and one whole wall was covered with family photographs. He pointed to one of my brother standing in front of the Eiffel Tower. He said, "I see that boy was in the 8th Air Force. Who is he and where was his squadron stationed?" "My brother, and Bury St. Edmond," I said. "I think he was either next to or near the Bloody 100th." The man slowly put down his tools and climbed down the ladder and looked at me and said, "Lady, how do you know about the Bloody 100th, for God's sake? I was in it." (A moment for explanations, if a B-17 bomber were in trouble or possibly the pilot didn't think it could get back to its field, it let down its landing gear which meant, "surrender." After the landing gear was lowered, German fighter planes would come to guide it to a German airfield and the crew was sent to POW camps. Once, however, a B-17 from the 100th let down its landing gear and two fighters came in to escort it, when suddenly every gun on the B-17 started to blaze and the fighters were shot down. Johnny thought it was a tragic ruse to hit more fighters.)

In a few minutes the plasterer and I were sitting, with cups of coffee at my kitchen table. He told me that the pilot of the B-17 had indeed made a drastic mistake! From then on the Germans waited for the 100th to fly, and their casualties were three times worse than any of the other squadrons.

Johnny had told me after the war that he didn't think security could have been any tighter, but someone had to have known when the 100th flew and informed the Germans.

The plasterer told me that that same afternoon. The crew of that ship were all sent to different airfields. "I was in that raid!"

I said, "No chance? The order to fire was a mistake?"

"None! And I'd give a lot to know how it happened." He scratched his head, "But the queer thing is your knowing that I was in the Bloody 100th!" He also related to me, "I was there. I saw it happen and I wanted to get out of that squadron more than anything in the world, but I had to finish my tour of duty with that squadron . . . but pretty soon we began to have thirty to forty percent more casualties than any other squadron in the area."

Johnny at the base of the Eiffel Tower in 1945.

Of Love and Leland 81

What would we have done without the radio, newspapers, and the telephone? Here is a word for all of you who take electronic gadgets for granted. It is about calling someone long distance in "olden times." In 1945 if you wanted to call long distance and if the circuits weren't all busy which they usually were, you dialed the long distance operator and told her what city you wanted to reach and what person you wanted to talk to. Station-to-station or person-to-person? I said, "Both in a way." She said in a resigned tone, "We'll begin with station-to-station." But in olden times, no robot told you, "You must dial a '1' or a '2' first." The telephone long distance operators probably had one of the hardest jobs in the world. If you were calling, you could hear the operator patching your call through, say, Chicago, then Denver, then Phoenix, and you could hear each operator speaking. And I had an especially difficult job making one call.

My brother was just about ready to go overseas. He had a three-day pass and had gone to visit friends, and we also knew that he was flying over a new B-17 for the 8th Air Force. My father was almost on the verge of collapse. He simply had to talk to Johnny before he went overseas, and Daddy usually kept a fairly calm demeanor, but not this time. I heard him muttering, "Judas priest! You're only a junior in high school. And you're navigating a bomber to England . . . when last year you couldn't even find Washington Street!" Then to me, "Susie, you'll have to find him for me. He did say in his letter that he was spending the weekend with Lt. Barth in Kansas City. You'll just have to find which Barth it is, and where Johnny is now. Susie, you have to do this for me." I said, "Okay, here it goes." So, I assumed an urgent tone, and said a lot of "pleases" and "if you could's," and when I finally got the Kansas City operator, I just had to tell her the whole story. That I had to find a family named Barth who entertained Lt. John Jameson the previous weekend. We even giggled together. The operator said, "What if his mother has remarried and has a different name?" I told her, "Don't even think that!" They were the unsung heroines and she said, "Well, hang up and in-between my other things, I'll keep trying the Barths and I'll call you when I get them."

About half an hour later, she called me triumphantly. "I found them when I dialed the fourteenth Barth. And I gave Mrs. Barth your telephone number." So, Mrs. Barth did call Daddy and he got a detailed report of Johnny.

Later, my father wrote to the president of the Kansas City telephone company and told him about his operator who had found the Barths for him. The result of this was that the operator was honored in the telephone company magazine, and the company gave her a raise.

☙ ☙ ☙

A couple of days later Mr. Parlette invited me to have lunch with him. This in itself was unusual, but I was pleased. After we were seated he said to me, "Susie, do you think you could run the Order Department?"

"Who, me? Well, I don't know. Yeah, I guess I could. But what about you? Where are you going?"

He said, "I'm resigning as of next Friday."

I said, "Why?"

"All the department heads have been told to buy stock in the Electronics Laboratories. After the war they plan to retool the plants to make expensive toys for children."

"I don't believe it. Do you think any of them knows one end of a toy train from another?" He laughed and said, "I think it is highly doubtful. I think I'm going to go back into selling. I was a good salesman before the war, and I supported my family on it. If you do resign in the future, I know that I will be keeping a small office here and maybe I could hire you to come down two or three mornings a week to keep the mail caught up. But not to call your friend Ann, not on my nickel." All of the war wives had known that something was up, but the toys we hadn't heard about yet.

"I'm probably not going to accept the offer for the job, but I'm very flattered. But now that the war in Europe is over and if Frank doesn't have to go to the Pacific, he might be coming home in the fall. That may be just wishful thinking, but a lot of us are doing it right now." I said to him, "You know, ever since that invoice and file on the black light were sitting on my desk and then in my file cabinet, I somehow haven't been able to take our contributions to the war effort very seriously. In fact, I think the whole plant sort of reminds me of an erector set put up by a crazy man."

He nodded. "I have met and talked with the man who will take my place, that is if you turn me down, and I have a hunch maybe you had better plan on resigning too. Whether Frank goes to the Pacific or not."

Mr. Parlette did quit and his replacement came in. I didn't like him from the moment I saw him and when I took my first couple of letters for dictation, I realized that I would have to improve on his grammar too. Then one afternoon he boasted about how he managed to get the status of being "indispensable." Then he followed this up with telling us how cleverly he cheated on his income tax.

The five people in the office were silent—ominously silent. Then I picked up the phone and asked Helen to get me the numbers of the IRS and the head of the Draft Board. Then I smiled at him and said, "See how easy it is to be an informer?" Hal Palen said seriously to him, "If she tells this to any one of the forty-four wives who run this place, you better start praying and running both, and get a head start."

I added, "And you don't say 'for you and I' to the vice president of the Electric Boat Company." I didn't know that I could fight so dirty. But maybe I'd always known how. Then I stood up and yelled, "I quit!" before he could say, "You're fired!"

And I left. The people in Purchasing clapped, but I didn't think it wise to go back for a curtain call. Our offices were separated by a thin beaver board partition and an open door. Then I heard Dorothy, the moonlighter, calling at me to wait a minute. She caught up with me and handed me my purse which I had forgotten in my fury. This was the first time she ever praised me. She said, "Well, old girl, that's what I call making the shit hit the fan. I didn't know you had it in you." She gave me a hug then turned back towards the office saying, "I gotta grab your typewriter before that bitch Doreen gets it."

Mr. Parlette called me at home that night and said that the new man had abandoned ship that afternoon. But I didn't go back.

After I had stopped working, I did some household chores to help out. One was even pleasurable, and it always happened on Friday. Mr. Kincaid's Meat Market at 56th and Illinois was open for about an hour, maybe an hour and a half. My mother and other old customers used to call Mr. Kincaid on Monday and say something like, "I have twenty-one meat stamps this week." And he would say, "That's fine, come in between nine and ten on Friday." Each customer who had called in took a camp stool or something to sit on and knitted and gossiped and talked about our people in the war before Mr. Kincaid unlocked the door. North Illinois was a wonderful place to exchange news and hear the latest gossip about our soldiers. All the meat packages were wrapped and marked with the customer's name, and he would say, "You owe me seven dollars and fifty cents (or whatever) and twenty-two meat stamps," and we got our already wrapped meat. We didn't have the slightest idea of what we were getting until we opened the package at home. It might be a rump roast, a thick slice of ham, occasionally a fish, or chickens in any and all shapes and sizes. Mr. Kincaid, unlike a lot of butchers during World War II, would have nothing to do with the black market. Once he sent me home with a duck and nothing has ever been baked with such awe and care. All four cooks were helping. We carved it into four portions so no one could eat more than the other and we all had an equal share. We trusted our lives to each other, but never our duck. Mr. Kincaid is now where he should be—in Heaven. I used to beg both of his sons to let us buy meat this way—"fix me a surprise." Mr. Kincaid also supplied us with oleo. Of course there wasn't any butter, and I don't think anybody will ever forget that oleo—in a cellophane type bag, closed all the way around and looking like white lard (which it probably was), and in the middle there was a great big circle of red coloring. You had to knead and knead the unopened package and you ended up with lard streaked with orange. It's terrible to have that be one of your main memories of World War II.

I have asked other people what was the first thing they thought of if you said "World War II." My main memory would probably be oleo and Christ Church on the Circle on D-Day. Then I changed it to seeing Frank waiting for me at the end of the war in the rain on the porch at "Green Acres." Other people have said they think of FDR first; another man told me Okinawa—no wonder he remembers that, it's where his ship was sunk out from under him.

The allied ships offshore from Okinawa during the American landings were taking a terrible beating. One radio operator allegedly sent the following message to the operator on a nearby ship. "Jesus Christ: The same yesterday, today, and forever." Some of the Japs were Kamikaze pilots. The Japanese during the summer of 1945 were training thirteen and fourteen-year-olds as Kamikaze pilots.

※　　　※　　　※

Summer of 1945 in Leland. Frank and Johnny were still overseas. We spent the summer, Mother and I, scrounging for food and Daddy, proving again that there were no flies on him, scrounging for gasoline. Each car was allowed legally three gallons of gas a week. How come we had enough gas to drive to Leland? Don't ask. While Mother and I made cottage cheese and bread (not for fun but because there was none to buy) in the kitchen, Daddy with Joe Schwarz as accomplice, figured out a real scam. You see, nobody had thought about or made into law the gas rationing of boats. They figured out the most complicated and strenuous way possible to get gas from Joe's pumps into our car at the cottage. I'm not sure why. Maybe they were afraid of the law—doubtful—or that someone else would blackmail them into letting him into the scam. To get the gas you first went into town through the channel in a four-horsepower outboard and docked by the Bird, put Joe's gas into cans and then into the engine, went back to the cottage in the boat, siphoned gas into other containers, lugged it up to the car and siphoned it in. Whew! This complicated maneuver usually was done in the evening. And this is how we got the gas to drive home.

Daddy said, "Joe will take any kind of a ration card in exchange for gas." I would guess this was only done for good friends.

Mother and I bicycled in for groceries. That M-22 hill is a you-know-what when you have a full basket of cans and groceries and bikes with balloon tires.

Daddy thought, of course, the best thing for a worried war wife was "take her fishing." And so we did, and the scenario never varied. First find Willkie and tie him up. He was the dog that followed Petie, a Springer Spaniel named Wendell Willkie. (If you wonder about his name, back to American history when Indiana's Wendell Willkie unsuccessfully ran against FDR for President of the United States in 1942.)

We'd row to Cemetery Point in that same Maine dory. Those boats were meant to last. No matter how hard we tried to incarcerate Willkie, he got loose and swam after us. He would swim up to the boat and put on an act that left us breathless from laughing. He went vertical in the water, panted heavily, closed his eyes, and yelled in his dogly voice, "Help me, I'm drowning." So we'd drag him into the boat where he shook himself hard, dowsing us with water. Then he either sat on the worm can or the opened tackle box. After this he went to the bow and piteously cried, or rather howled, "Let's go home." Willkie was a canine Houdini, also a marvelous actor.

In the summer of 1945 we needed some laughs, and Willkie supplied them.

Because Petie and Willkie, my childhood dogs, spent more time in the water than on land, in later years I was very cross at the Mayberrys' landlubber dogs, Snoopy, Charlie and Gabby. When Frank took Charlie to Lake Michigan, he ran back to the car before he even saw the water. Once when Gabby, our black poodle, and I were on the dock, I pushed her into the water. As she swam to the shore, she gave me a look of deep reproach for my treachery. What's more, she never again came down to the dock if I were there.

In the afternoons when Daddy and I didn't go fishing, Mother and I bicycled down to the Joyes' beach. We'd take cottage cheese and be given jelly they'd put up. As we sat on the beach, there was one subject of conversation—FOOD. This must sound awfully tame, but we had to do something besides worry. We never discussed the war at all, but we instinctively knew which person was the most worried. That was the one summer we jammed into the post office before the mail was even sorted, everyone praying for letters from overseas. I usually was first in line. Frank was still worried he might be sent to the Pacific Theatre.

Occasionally Nincie Joyes Northcutt and her small son Allen bicycled down in the afternoon to borrow the rowboat to catch the fish for the pan that night. Ordinarily any of us would have thrown back the perches and rock bass, but not in 1945. Nincie used to laugh about her mother. When presented with the fish, Mrs. Joyes would sniff and say, "They're barely dead."

Then Mr. Joyes would reply, "That's what's called 'fresh fish.'"

The Joyes Cottage had by far the best books to borrow, wonderful old mysteries, probably all out of print now. Leland had no library then.

The Smith Cottage, on the other hand, had one book. Sally Smith used to sigh and say, "Well, I guess I'll have to read the *Diary of a Confederate Girl* again." However, you don't need a book to enjoy yourself in the Smith Cottage. Just look around. On the walls are: one, a map of the Maginot Line, circa 1938, and two, a profile on paper on another wall of Moby Dick, the huge bass Charlotte caught in Little Traverse Lake. She named him and he was cooked in a woodburning stove. Charlotte wouldn't have any other kind, and he fed twelve people. I know because I was one of them. Behind the front door was a dog leash of Charlotte's first dog, and some wooden golf clubs. She claimed she planted the acorn which is now the huge oak tree in the front yard.

One afternoon in July, 1945, Charlotte arrived by bicycle in her best dress and a basket full of gin and vermouth. "After the war," she said, "I'm going to have a huge Lawn Fete, but I feel that we should have a rehearsal right now."

During that same summer of 1945, Mother and I poked around in the Fish Room until we found what we wanted—the old-fashioned ice cream freezer, covered with dust and spiderwebs. And we made honest-to-goodness the most delicious homemade peach ice cream in the whole world. Johnny wasn't there to fight with me over who got to lick the paddles, and of course that made me both happy and sad.

V-J DAY—August, 14, 1945

If you asked any war wife who had a husband in Europe or in the Pacific what she thought about the Atomic Bomb, you'd get the same answer. I think the answer might be the same today, given the right circumstances, but the older I get the more I wonder whether in the Garden of Eden Eve stole the apple or plutonium.

Daddy and Joe Schwarz spent V-J Day night together sitting on the curb of his gas station. They drank a quart of whiskey from the bottle. That night was not the night for amenities like glasses and ice. Joe told Daddy a secret no summer person knew about, only Leland natives — a trout pond. It's near Lake Leelanau, but you can't find it from the road. He swore Daddy to secrecy. Daddy was up, off and running the next day. He claimed the trout jumped into his creel. Joe's revelation that night was one of true love. Daddy had to fish that pond at odd hours Joe had told him. If a native fisherman saw him, Daddy and Joe could be lynched.

လ လ လ

The war was over, really over, and a chapter closed, one that could never be approximated again. I don't understand everything that's going on today and I don't think I want to. I only know who we were.

Sentiments like these sound as if I am very cross at all the younger generations that followed mine. I'm really not—and I don't mean to preach. I'm just telling you the way it was. And don't forget, I've already said "we are a grouchy bunch," we women of World War II, at least I am, and I wished I'd been braver than I was.

Every once in a while, I used to hear a young wife say, "Well, if there were a war, I just wouldn't let Jim go, that's all there is to it." I just smile and think how far apart we generations are. We still carry a lot of baggage. Maybe we can't get rid of it, or maybe we don't want to. I did not distinguish myself as a war wife, but I did the best I could. If millions of people have the same total commitment to do the best they can, a war gets won.

How do you feel if you have been part of something that you were pretty sure was impossible? You are proud! Proud of yourself! Proud of your husband! And proud of your country! So, the peaceniks and revisionists can pack it up and go away. We have already made our history. America bent on imperialist revenge when the bomb was dropped? Preposterous! It would be blasphemy to the white crosses all over the globe to allow such hypocrisy to occur. You rewrite our history at your peril!

At the Fiftieth Anniversary of D-Day in 1994, some of the men, now old, made parachute jumps just as they had fifty years ago, the night before D-Day. Maybe they were in Harry's group. I heard and read what some people said about them. "The damned old fools, showing off.... lucky they didn't kill themselves." Maybe they would think, "What a way to go!" "Heroes and heroines" of the sixties never saw a cause worth fighting for. Some of these poor idiots don't even know the dates of World War II. The old men who did the parachuting did so because they just had to do it! To repeat the courage and excitement and danger that was the most important part of their lives.

One man broke his leg, and he must have been called "an old fool," and maybe worse, but I bet he just smiled. So. Was all the fear and the sacrifice and the loneliness worth it? I'll leave that for each woman to decide.

One day in November, 1945, I answered the telephone and I heard a voice say, "Hi, honey! I'm home." This was the greeting Frank used when he came home to our house in Joplin. Joplin had been such a long time ago. I said, "Are you really? Promise?" I marveled through my tears that I recognized his voice, but I still thought it might be some terrible joke. So I said, "Talk some more so I really know it's you" ... the rest of our forty-five minute conversation has been censored.

Our own V-J Day was November 12, 1945. We had said goodbye in the rain on a dark cold night, and I drove to Camp Atterbury on just such a night to get him. "What if we don't recognize each other?" "What if he doesn't like me?" "What if I don't like him?" We had such a little time together, what will I do if... what if? What if? What if? As I drove to the building where Frank had said he would be, I saw a soldier in an overcoat, hat on the back of his head, and he was trying to shield his eyes from the rain as he peered down the street. I honked the horn, jumped out of the car, leaving the engine running, the door wide open, and the headlights and wipers still on. And I ran. And Frank ran. He whirled me around and I think we just shouted for joy. Raindrops and teardrops. We had been so far apart for so long, and coming together again seemed to be a miracle. I think we laughed and laughed. How would I know whether the war years were worth it or not? I was having my breath squeezed out of me and I was experiencing JOY!

And soon summer would come again.

༄ ༄ ༄

I wasn't home when Frank arrived at Leland for the first time. When I returned, he was standing on the porch looking at the lake, an untouched drink in his hand. "Why didn't you tell me it was so beautiful?" he asked. Now I really knew why I loved him.

Frank had a couple of interesting fishing trips with my father the first year he came up. They were out by the old red barn, gone now, when the sheriff came up to the boat to see their fishing licenses. Of course, Frank didn't have one. Also, he had caught a very nice bass and my father quickly said, "That's my fish." He didn't want that nice bass confiscated.

Mother and I were enjoying life in the front yard about noon as the sheriff towed them home in disgrace. Mother, when she saw the boat said, "Aren't we lucky? They've broken down and that nice man is bringing them home." That was a very expensive fish. I think a twenty dollar fine and ten dollars for a fishing license was the extent of it.

Another time, much more fun for Frank, was another fishing trip with Daddy. Daddy always insisted that there be a chair in the boat, and I quote, "because of my damned piles." I kind of remember its being a director's chair, but I'm not sure. Somehow or other Daddy leaned back too far and he somersaulted backwards into the lake, taking the chair and his rod with him.

Frank said he came to the surface slowly doing the breast stroke gently and blowing spouts of water out of his mouth; his glasses and his hat still on. Frank was in such a state of helpless hysteria that it was quite a while before he could help his father-in-law into the boat, and then he caught hell from Daddy for laughing so hard. Daddy sputtered "You damned little bird!" He had lost his rod, but believe it or not, they got the chair and rod up with Frank's line and hook.

Now somehow Frank was under the impression that his father-in-law had fragile health. On the other hand, Frank, just out of the Army was supposedly still very fit. One day Daddy invited Frank for a day's trout fishing on the Boardman River about an hour's drive from Leland. A day on the Boardman meant just that, "a DAY." The fishermen took lunch, sandwiches, coffee, whiskey, or whatever, stored in the huge pockets of waders. They drove and drove, and driving with my father was an unnerving experience to begin with. Then they walked and walked in their waders and all the equipment. In the river Frank was left entirely on his own while my father went upstream. It was a cold, cloudy day, the river was very high and the current was swift. He had also been left in a deep place. What's more, he had never cast a fly in his life. He lost his flies in over-hanging branches and he never even had a strike. Light years of misery later, here came Daddy, happy with a creel full of little beauties. More walking, more driving. Frank did just manage to stay awake during the dinner. Then he fell onto his bed in the last stages of exhaustion, so tired he didn't even put on his pajamas. His frail father-in-law had had a nice dip in the lake and he and Mother went off for an evening of bridge, Daddy in fine fettle. Here ended any ideas Frank might have heard about Daddy's frailties.

Not only did Daddy spend all the time he could in the summer fishing, he never missed the opening of the trout season in Michigan, May first. The summer purists weren't around the first week in May. Worms were used. And they often fished in the snow. When we had been little, children had orders to be in the driveway of 4401 Broadway as he drove in and yell, "Have you?" He always had. He arrived very hung over, exhausted, triumphant and with big fish. Once I caught hell from him when I asked him what a big gash was doing on a fish. It was gaffed, that's what. The native kids made good money gaffing fish and selling them to fishermen who weren't catching many, or so I was told. I began to feel sorry for the poor mother trout who just wanted to lay her eggs in peace and got gaffed for her maternal instincts.

When I pressed Daddy on how he managed on these strenuous trips, he said, "I live on whiskey, eggs and Amytol, just as I do at Princeton reunions." It seems to have been a good combination, if unusual.

One of my favorite memories of my father was the sight of him in Leland trolling every calm night. He was after that mythical huge lake trout no one ever caught. Very slowly the boat stitched its way to Cemetery Point as he played out his line from his tippy chair. On some calm nights the lake looked like pewter as the sun set over Lake Michigan and he turned into a silhouette in the dusk. Ichabod Crane with a fishing cap on.

I've been wondering about the fishing mystique and how I might define the passion for fishing that my father had. And I think passion is probably the right word. Is it passed through the genes? Well, Johnny used to love fishing. A fisherman friend of mine says, "It can be caught." Maybe the way Daddy caught it was from Althea and Julie Brooks, and Mr. Charles Culp caught it from Daddy during a Leland visit after which they built their own cottage on Lake Michigan. I should think that there is no cure and no inoculation that works. Also, that you have to be especially fond of the person you introduce to trout fishing. Anyway, I don't think the love of fishing can be readily defined. All I have found in the looking for a definition is the following. It's more than a definition, but it's nice.

Fishing is worth any amount of effort and expense to people who love it, because in the end you can get such a large number of dreams per fish. You can dream about a fish for years before the one moment when your fly is in the right place, and when something is about to happen, when you hold your breath and time expands like a bubble until suddenly fish and fisherman feel each other's life weight. And for a long time afterward the memory of that moment gives you something you can rest your mind on just before you sleep.

I think you take a chance when you introduce a dear friend to one of your special joys. I'm talking about trout fishing, but it could just as well be a poem, a piece of music, a sermon, a view. And if your friend instantaneously shares in what you love, you will have what C.S. Lewis says is ". . . a brief glimpse into heaven," a present God gives to some of us on our earthly journey. If your friend does not share your love, you never like him less. You must think, or I think you think, "It would have been so wonderful if only . . .."

Daddy took such a chance when he introduced Mr. Culp to trout fishing. Some sort of a heart-to-heart wave length occurred, and the bond was never broken. I will never believe that this bond occurred because of the Jameson-Culp weekly bridge games. Their gentle communion occurred because they loved to fish together.

Once Daddy asked Mr. Culp to join him and his friends during the opening week of the trout season in Michigan. After Daddy had partially recovered from his strenuous and alcoholic week, Mother asked him, "Do you think Charlie had a good time?"

His answer was, "I've never in my whole life seen a man have so much fun."

In 1963 Mr. Culp died very suddenly from a heart attack. Daddy was in the hospital then, gravely ill, and Johnny had to tell his father about it. Johnny reported that after he had told him, Daddy turned his head away from Johnny and said through tears, "I loved Charlie Culp." I hope it's not too much to believe that they are together catching their limit in heavenly trout streams.

Daddy's fishing hat was rarely off his head. One day in town someone mistook him for a native. He didn't quite know whether to be flattered or not, but decided he was flattered. This was long before you were supposed to say, "Leland persons," or whatever, a silly euphemism, I think. I don't mind being called a native of Indianapolis, but someone I think thought "natives" was pejorative.

Sometime in the late forties, Mr. and Mrs. McPharen Barr, from Louisville, bought the "Old" Taylor Cottage, a couple of doors north of the Joyes. It was practically derelict, it was in such terrible shape. He spent a great deal of money on it and the result was a lovely place. One day Mr. Barr and Daddy were sitting on the curb in front of the Merc while their ladies shopped. This was about fifteen years after Mr. Barr had bought his cottage.

"John," he said wistfully, "Will our cottage always be called 'The Taylor Cottage?'"

"Sure will," said his native friend. "But somebody might say, 'The Taylor Cottage has been spruced up a bit.'"

It may still be called that, though Mr. and Mrs. Barr have died.

ঔ ঔ ঔ

In time, our two daughters joined the Leland generation. Of course, Susie doesn't remember her first or second trip to Leland. The first was with my father who picked us up at about three in the morning. After about three hours of squirming and crying, Susie went to sleep. Then the beautiful sun came up. My father turned around, woke her up to watch it. She was eleven months old and I'm sure she was charmed. Finally she went to sleep again. Then we stopped at the place where he picked up night crawlers. He always got enough for the whole summer and they lived in spanghum moss in a huge can in the pump house, so, of course, she woke up again. Susie was now awake for the rest of the time.

In the vicinity of Cadillac, Michigan, water began to leak from the exhaust pipe. My father would drive about five miles and then we would stop and pour in water. It seems that the car had a cracked block. Cars broke down a lot more often in olden times. With the engine about to explode from no water, and steam pouring out, we got to the top of the hill by Northfields. Daddy pushed his foot to the floor and said grimly, "Come on, you bastard." The bastard did as commanded. Daddy always drove like a race driver. He used to say, "Sixty miles, sixty minutes," and he almost made it.

The summer after second daughter Kit was born in May of 1950, she stayed home with Mrs. Bicknell (R.I.P.) and lots of TLC, and Susie and I went up to Leland on the Pullman. Susie had a ball; her mother did not. Only a fool takes a two-year old to the dining car. She crumpled crackers and spilled the milk, naturally. And as we started out of the car, she grabbed a chicken leg from a plate on another table and ran squealing and waving it straight into the dining car kitchen. These are probably three or four feet wide with stoves along each side. She and a waiter carrying boiling soup nearly collided. This gentleman almost turned white with horror. Apologies all around from an embarrassed mother.

❧   ❧   ❧

We went to Leland with Mother the year my father died (June 1963). It was not an easy summer for any of us. One day Mother and Aunt Harris, a widow of some years, were sitting on the front porch. I was in the living room and I heard Mother say, "I'm even more lonely because the Mayberrys are here. They're a whole family and they don't need me at all. In fact, nobody needs me."

I'm still mad at myself. I should have gone right out on the porch and given Mother a big hug and said the right things. Well, there aren't any "right things" to say, but I could have said how much we loved her and needed her. Sometimes I think of that during the Episcopal Confession, "We have left undone those things which we ought to have done . . ." Why didn't I go out to her? I don't know. In our family there was lots of love, but not much overt affection. We didn't do what my daughter Kit used to say when she was little, "Let's hug and kiss and pat." A pat on the shoulder from my father was a sign of great affection.

Kit and I share a special memory of him that happened that summer. She and Daddy used to have an amiable argument every morning after it had rained. How much money should he give her for bailing the boat. A dime? Fifty cents? The amount was renegotiated after every rain. Kit went to the dock one morning to bail and I was sitting in the front yard. She was thirteen that summer. As I idly watched her and the lake, my father was suddenly THERE beside me. I don't expect anyone to believe me, and I don't care whether anyone does or not. I didn't see him or hear him. I just knew he was there and as a happy spirit checking us out. Do you think, "She was just remembering him and imagined it?" NO, HE WAS THERE. It may just be one of the most important instants in my life. I kept thinking, "Talk to me," but he didn't. In a minute or so Kit tore up the dock steps like a scalded cat, saying "Boppy's on the dock."

"I know it," I said. "He was just here in the yard." I forget what else we said, but I suggested we not tell anybody else. I waited for him to come back again, but he didn't. I'm hoping after I die I can check in with the people of Leland, but since I don't know the drill yet, I'm not sure.

∽   ∽   ∽

Mother died on July 31, 1977. There was a memorial service in Indianapolis in the chapel of Second Presbyterian Church. "The Brother James Air" we had learned at choir practice in Leland was sung again. There was a second service that Mother would have loved in the front yard of the cottage. I wasn't there, but Babe said it was a beautiful day. All the Millers, Pawlicks, Duttons, Mary Anthony and maybe a few more were there. Her son-in-law, Tid, read Bible messages, and they said The Lord's Prayer. Then they toasted Granny with Bloody Marys. She would have loved it. The Leland front yard was her favorite place in the world, I think. Perhaps she was there, too, as my father had been earlier.

Babe and I inherited the cottage from Mother. Johnny took his third in cash. Frank and I went up in July and Babe rented the cottage in August. We never had a lot of fun; in fact, often no fun at all. One reason was my health. Another one was that we didn't have a boat. Right after Daddy died, Mother sold the boat for fifty dollars. Babe may have gotten over her fury about this by now, but I'm not sure. She doesn't really believe me when I say Daddy never let Susie and Kit use it. Just as her children were grown up enough to use it, it wasn't there anymore. We missed it more than the Miller kids did, I think. My feeling is that a day when you aren't on the lake or in it is a wasted day.

When we were in charge of the cottage in July, it seemed to me that we spent an awful lot of time working instead of vacationing. Get new sheets, replace screens, order wood, take trips to the hardware store, get rid of wasps nests, cut the grass and trim the bushes and change locks. You name it, we did it.

We did not, however, "weed the myrtle," by the dock steps, a joke among all of us. Mother seemed always to be weeding myrtle. I had the myrtle dug up and replaced with grass. Kit and Tim transplanted lots of it to the front yard, and Tim fixed the garbage can box so the most ingenious raccoon in the world couldn't get in.

One year I had to fire the "Green Acres" caretaker and find another one. I called Mr. Donald Dunklow. He did not say "Yes," but he said he and Mrs. Dunklow would call on us that evening. We slicked up ourselves and the cottage. We sat around chatting while they looked it and us over. We passed. They are special people. If Mr. Dunklow says he'll do something, he does it—a somewhat unusual quality today.

Frank and I often walked down to Dick and Mary Capps' for a drink. And we truly coveted that perfect little cottage. We'd come home and decide what should be done to "Green Acres." Pure fantasy. All windows made larger, make the far end of the dining room and Cora's (our summer cook) room and the little junk room into a really nice bedroom and bathroom with a shower. Make the stairs have a landing. Start up from the swinging door into the kitchen.

Once Gene Miller, my nephew-contractor, had come over in reply to an SOS to keep us from having a fire due to some bad wiring. He wouldn't let us turn on a light till the next day when he came down with Mr. Bunek, the expert. We were having a beer in the dark and I mentioned our plans for the house. I couldn't see in the dark whether Gene's hair had turned white or not, but he said, oh, so seriously, "Aunt Susie, for God's sake, just forget it. If you even lean on a bearing wall, the whole cottage might fall down."

Of course, he was right. One should not tinker with a sixty-year-old cottage that cost $2,600 to build.

The first year after Mother's death, Frank and I cleaned out the cottage to get it ready for renters, and too, just to get rid of the loads of stuff, some of which had been there since the cottage was built. We never threw away anything we outgrew, just jammed it somewhere. Four bureaus had nothing but old bathing suits. We could have outfitted either sex in any size. My favorite coat was a raincoat Mother wore in bad weather. It came to her ankles. I think it belonged to my Grandfather Hanckel, her own father.

When we had rainy weather, whoever was going out just reached into that pitch dark closet under the stairs and grabbed a coat—any coat. Often we didn't know whose it was. We were a family of five, but the closet, I think, had eight or ten raincoats, all hung on two long nails. You grabbed the one on top. This usually caused the others to fall down.

Daddy used to say, "I'm opposed to all change, even if it's for the better." I'm inclined to agree with him where Leland clothes are concerned. No one now seems to wear those marvelous old clothes that lived all year in the cottage. The mice liked them, too.

There was a huge church rummage sale that year, so we just piled stuff in the back yard. One day I took out Daddy's trout rod and tips from Hardys in London, his most cherished possessions. Then I took out my Grandfather Hanckel's huge tackle box, the one always filled with tools that lived under the kitchen shelf. Then I came into the cottage and burst into tears. I retrieved the rod and tips and tackle box and put them in the Fish Room. I couldn't handle the things in Mom's desk, so Frank did that for me.

When I realized I could not handle the expenses and hassles of being a cottage owner, I went up to Leland alone in June of 1983. I knew in my mind what I was going to do, hand it over to Susie and Kit. But I guess I needed to know it in my heart.

The weather was glorious and I had a wonderful time all by myself. I used to take my coffee out to the front yard about seven in the morning and watch the chippies and hear the birds and remember happy times. Jack Gilligan and Katie took me out a couple of times as did Pres Joyes. I think Jack knew what I was doing. The last night I was there he kissed me goodbye and said, "It's still yours in every way that matters," and he was right. There's a golden oldie whose refrain is, "Oh, they can't take that away from me."

That week I was getting the cottage ready for Tucker Hawkins, of Indianapolis, and his family to rent. He says he still has the list of things I made about the cottage. For instance, "If the bathroom light won't go on when you flip the switch, just put your finger up on the fluorescent bulb on the ceiling and then it will. NEVER open a window without putting a stick under the bottom part. That is, don't do it unless you want a broken hand."

I spoiled the Hawkinses for life. I left food for dinner and breakfast in the refrigerator and a bottle of whiskey on the bar. My only request: "Don't use Daddy's fly rod or his fishing hat on a nail in the dining room."

He called me the night they arrived. The children had already been to the Bloody Ghost Tree. I'd told them where it was. He was renting our caretaker's boat and everything was wonderful. One morning he called to say, "We lost some trees in a big storm, but I've called Mr. Dunklow and he'll take care of them." If an owner had been in residence, those trees would still be lying there.

Later that summer there was "Nana's Folly" Weekend, worth every penny and fun! Gosh! I've never had such fun. It was a lead-in to our 1984 vacation. I flew up in a private plane two hours from Indianapolis to Traverse where I rented a car. I stayed at Falling Waters. What was the urgency? I had five grandchildren on the same beach, and that's urgent! The Quills were in the Miller Cottage. No cooking, my kids took me out, I played with the grandchildren. In fact, it was perfect.

An added serendipity happened as I was eating lunch one day at the Cove. Someone tapped me on the shoulder. Mary Bruce Cobb! She and I had been soul mates since we were born. We had a very special afternoon in front of the Bruce Cottage next to the Miller Cottage. We sat a little ways from the lake and watched both sets of our grandchildren playing on the beach and in the water, just as our parents had watched us so long ago. This in a nutshell, is what Leland is all about.

Our children, the Quills, Meads and I had a glorious morning in our front yard. The August renters didn't like it and left. This was the yard as it always should be—naked babies, Nana, wet towels, confusion and lots of laughing. BEDLAM!

The "Skinny-Mini" was overflowing and water was starting to trickle from Cora's room up above onto the kitchen floor, but no one gave a darn.

I thought it would be so great to take my five granddaughters to the Sunday Night Sing. First we ate at the Blue Bird, at considerable expense because all ate a lot. Then Edie said, "Gimmie five dollars quick, Nana!"

"What for?"

"I gotta get our ice cream next door to eat in the car." Nana obliged though the Sing didn't live up to expectation.

In 1984, June and part of July, Frank and I had our PERFECT VACATION. Falling Waters again. These ten days more than made up for some of our less happy Julys. I never felt sick, I never went to the doctor, I never took a pill, I never made a list, I never cooked. We played golf every day at eight AM and the back nine was ours. The Quills were in the cottage and we went and visited with them after golf. Weather perfect. Frank loved golf and that is my BEST UNHEARD OF SERENDIPITY!

The little girls and I shopped nearly every day. More of the tinkling of the cash register as "Jesus Saves." The Thunderbird, just out of Lake Leelanau, had a new huge sign, "The King is Coming." He didn't while we were there.

We had a memorable dinner at the Bird. Babe, who had just arrived, joined us and the Quills came by boat. Carrie and I had discussed our costumes for the evening, and we both wore "our blues" at her suggestion. Kit looked across the table and said, "I see three pairs of brown eyes all in a row." Guess whose? The little girls insisted on being both beside their Aunt Babe, whom they love very dearly.

They were both terribly concerned when we went to the Miller Cottage. She turned on the faucet and it sounded as if a helicopter were landing on the roof. There again, water trouble. Time for a new pump.

Another memorable time for me anyway, was when Megan and I were wading around at the bottom of the dock looking for crawdads, just as Julie Brooks Cunningham had done with the three Jamesons. Meggie looked up at me with those round blue eyes, "You're awful old, Nana, but you're awful nice."

When I count my blessings, I realize that Leland is a bright thread running through my life. When I think of the term, "Clouds of Witnesses," Hebrews, I think of my Leland family and friends I've loved and will never forget.

I like to think of them looking down on all at the little town by the falling waters and wishing everybody joy.

THE GENERATIONS—A PHOTO RECOLLECTION

Grandchildren enjoy a spring day on the beach at Leland.

The yard at "Green Acres" has seen many youngsters from the 1920s on. Here we are with daughters Susie and Kit.

My father always looked forward to the opening day of trout fishing where he had his fill of "whiskey, eggs, and amytol."

Frank and I introduced the fourth generation to the joys "Of Love and Leland" at "Green Acres."

Frank and Tippy.

My mother Florence Jameson was the first of our family to see Leland (1913).
1945 photo